For Ellen

THANKS
for the
TROUBLE

Also by Tommy Wallach

WE ALL LOOKED UP

TOMMY WALLACH

THANKS
for the
TROUBLE

SIMON & SCHUSTER

First published in Great Britain in 2016 by Simon & Schuster UK Ltd
A CBS COMPANY

Originally published in the USA in 2016 by Simon & Schuster BFYR,
an imprint of Simon & Schuster Children's Publishing Division,
1230 Avenue of the Americas, New York, NY 10020

1 3 5 7 9 10 8 6 4 2

Simon & Schuster UK Ltd
1st Floor, 222 Gray's Inn Road
London
WC1X 8HB

www.simonandschuster.co.uk

Simon & Schuster Australia, Sydney
Simon & Schuster India, New Delhi

A CIP catalogue record for this book
is available from the British Library.

PB ISBN 978-1-4711-4612-1
eBook ISBN 978-1-4711-4613-8

Printed and bound by CPI Group (UK) Ltd, Croydon, CR0 4YY

Simon & Schuster UK Ltd are committed to sourcing paper
that is made from wood grown in sustainable forests and supports the Forest
Stewardship Council, the leading international forest certification organisation.
Our books displaying the FSC logo are printed on FSC certified paper.

MY LOVE, IF I DIE AND YOU DON'T—,

My love, if you die and I don't—,
let's not give grief an even greater field.
No expanse is greater than where we live.

Dust in the wheat, sand in the deserts,
time, wandering water, the vague wind
swept us like sailing seeds.
We might not have found one another in time.

This meadow where we find ourselves,
O little infinity! we give it back.
But Love, this love has not ended:

just as it never had a birth, it has
no death: it is like a long river,
only changing lands, and changing lips.

—*Pablo Neruda*

FRIDAY, OCTOBER
31

THIRD PERSON FAIL

THE BOY SAT ON A BENCH IN THE LOBBY of the Palace Hotel. It was about eight thirty in the morning, and he was supposed to be at school. But the boy had always thought it was a load of BS that you were expected to go to school on Halloween, so he'd decided not to. Maybe he'd go later. Maybe not. At this stage, it didn't really make much of a difference either way.

The boy noticed he was drawing more attention than he usually did. He'd been to the Palace plenty of times before, but this was the first time he'd shown up on a weekday, and the place wasn't busy enough for someone like him to go unremarked. He was dressed in dirty jeans and an old black T-shirt, and his hair was long and probably a mess (full disclosure: he hadn't looked in the mirror before leaving the house that morning). Also, he was Latino, which made him one of the very few Latino people in the building who wasn't there to bring room service to or clean up the dishes of or mop up the floors for old, rich, white people. To put it bluntly, he looked like he'd come there with some sort of criminal intention, which was racist and judgmental and totally non-PC.

It was also true.

That's not to say that the boy looked like a thug. He was just your average teenager. Or a little above average, actually. Like, you'd probably think he was cute, if you had to weigh in one way or the other. Or not cute, maybe, but not *not* cute either. Just, like, your normal level of cuteness. A solid seven out of ten. Maybe a B/B+ on a good day, in the right light, taking the most forgiving possible position on his too-thick eyebrows and his weirdly prominent dimples when he smiled and his slight butt chin . . .

Fuck me. This is turning into a disaster, isn't it?

I thought it would be better to write this in the third person, to give myself a little critical perspective. But it feels pretty messed up to write about whether I'm cute while pretending I'm not the one writing about whether I'm cute. It would be like writing your own recommendation letter or something.

Shit. I just noticed I used the *F* word up there. Oh, and now I've written "shit." I guess I could go back and delete them, but I'd rather not. I mean, do we really have to play this game, where because I'm who I am and you're who you are, we pretend that the word "fuck" doesn't exist, and while we're at it, that the action that underlies the word doesn't exist, and I just puke up a bunch of junk about how some teacher *changed my life* by teaching me how Shakespeare was actually the world's first rapper, or about the time I was doing community service with a bunch of homeless teenagers dying of cancer or something and felt the *deep* call of selfless action, or else I pull out all the stops and give you the play-by-play sob story of what happened to my dad, or some other terrible heartbreak of a thing that makes you feel so bummed out you figure, what the hell, we've got quotas after all, and this kid's gotten screwed over enough, so you give me the big old stamp of approval and a fat envelope in the mail come April?

I say no. I say let's not play games. You asked me a question—*What was the single most important experience of your life?*—and I'm going to answer it, even though my answer might be a little longer than five hundred words and might have the *F* word in it, and even the *F* action in it, and a whole lot of other stuff I'd have to be crazy to put down on paper and send to you. And then you'll read my answer, and you'll make your decision.

Let's start over.

Nice to meet you. I'm Parker Santé. I am medium cute, and bad at writing in the third person. Here is how the most important experience of my life began.

PERFECT

THERE IS SUCH A THING AS PERFECT
sadness. I know, because I've seen it.

People usually use that word—"perfect"—to talk about good things: a perfect score on a test, or a perfect attendance record, or landing a perfect 1080. But I think it's a way better word when it's used to describe something—even a totally shitty something—that's exactly the thing it's supposed to be. Perfect morning breath. A perfect hangover. Perfect sadness.

I was sitting on a bench in the lobby of the Palace Hotel. From there, I could see everything that went on: rich people checking in, rich people checking out, and through the stone arches beyond the reception desk, rich people nibbling and sipping away in the dining room. Have you ever been to the dining room of the Palace? It's got this crazy-high ceiling, all green metal and frosted glass, ribbed like the dried-out carcass of a big old whale with wrought-iron bones. People sit at these long communal tables that are basically fancier versions of the cafeteria tables we have at school. Each place setting has a collection of different-size forks tucked into napkins—a creepy little fork family sharing a single fork bed. Waiters scurry around like penguin parents who've lost their penguin babies.

"You can leave that. I'm enjoying playing with it."

Her voice cut through the background rustle and murmur of the room, as if she were sitting right next to me. My ears got stuck on her, the way your clothes sometimes catch on brambles when you're picking blackberries, so that you feel you might tear something if you pull away too quickly. I scoured the room for her, but it wasn't until she spoke again that I found her. She was sitting at the end of one of the communal tables, talking to a waiter.

"No, I'm not staying at the hotel. I'll just pay in cash."

She reached into her purse and pulled out the fattest stack of hundreds I'd ever seen in real life. I'm talking a hip-hop video kind of wad, thick as a John Grisham paperback. She peeled off one of the bills—(I see you, Mr. Franklin)—and handed it over. "Keep the change," she said. The waiter nodded a stunned little bobblehead nod, then peeled out before the girl could think better of her generosity, leaving her to tap idly at the top of a soft-boiled egg in an elaborate silver eggcup. I stared at her staring off into space, and counted the many ways in which she was incredible.

#1: She looked my age, or maybe a tiny bit older. Unless you're a hotelophile like myself, you're probably unaware of the fact that there is a direct correlation between the age of a hotel and the age of its average guest. The Palace is the oldest hotel in San Francisco, which means the dining room usually looks like some kind of swanky assisted-living facility. But this teenage girl had come in here to eat breakfast all on her own.

#2: She was pretty. I couldn't tell how pretty yet, because I was far away, but far away was still close enough. Certain people just shine.

#3: She wore a look of perfect sadness on her face.

#4: She had silver hair. At first I thought it was just a trick of the light, but then she shook her head, as if trying to shake off a bad memory, and it was like a thousand strands of tinsel shivering in a breeze.

#5: She had crazy money.

I stood up and went into the dining room, sitting down a couple of seats away from her at the same table. And yeah, I'd been right: pretty. Maybe even beautiful, though that word kinda makes me wanna throw up. When the waiter came over, I pointed at where it said "coffee" on the menu ($4.50 for a drip, and *I'm* the one at risk of being arrested for petty theft?).

"That's all?" he asked.

I nodded.

"Cream and sugar?"

I shook my head.

"Very good. Back in a moment."

Out of the corner of my eye, I watched the girl continue to mash the top of her egg. It didn't seem like she was going anywhere anytime soon, and I'd look suspicious just sitting there doing nothing, so I took out my journal and began to make up a story. I was only trying to pass the time until an opportune moment to lift the wad presented itself, but before I knew it, I ended up totally distracted by what I was writing. This happens to me sometimes. Once, I got this really great idea right at the beginning of a geometry class, and the next time I looked up from my notebook, the class had ended. I was the only person left in the room other than the teacher.

"How's it coming?" he'd asked.

I don't know how long I spent caught up in the story I wrote that day at the Palace, but when I placed the final period at the end of the last sentence and shut the front cover, I realized I hadn't checked up on the silver-haired girl for a *long* time. I glanced over at where she'd been sitting and experienced two powerful and contradictory emotions at once.

Despair, because she was gone.

And elation, because her purse was not.

GOOD EGGS AND BAD EGGS

YOU'D THINK I STARTED HANGING OUT IN hotels because they're a great place to rip people off, but it actually happened the other way around. I've always loved hotels. I love their unapologetic hotel-ness. All hotels looks like all other hotels. All hotels smell like all other hotels. All hotel food tastes like all other hotel food. Someone could show you a picture of a room, anywhere in the world, and you'd immediately know if it was a hotel room or a normal room. There's a sameness that transcends branding—Ramada or Hilton, Doubletree or Motel 6—as if every hotel were actually the same hotel, connected via wormhole across space and time. They all share the same flowery bedspreads with the crunchy texture of an unwashed gym class T-shirt, the carpeting that is almost (but not quite) dark enough to mask the full extent of its foulness, and art of such insistent and offensive blandness that it makes each guest feel as if he has been committed to a mental institution that believes he poses a danger to himself and must therefore be pacified via watercolor landscape painting.

If I ever owned a hotel, I think it would be cool to try and make it so that no one could actually tell it was a hotel. I could put a row of busted-up sneakers just inside the door of every room, and a couple of used toothbrushes in a glass above every bathroom sink, and pack every closet full of old coats and boxes and board games missing critical pieces. My guests would wake up thinking they were waking up at a friend's house, or maybe even their own. Then they'd go downstairs into the kitchen and pour themselves a bowl of cereal from the half-empty box of stale Frosted Mini-Wheats placed there by my staff every morning.

Of course, a hotel like that wouldn't be very useful to a kid like me, from a thievery point of view, because people would treat it the same way they treated their homes. And homeowners are always careful. They lock the doors and set the alarms. They're on the lookout for suspicious activity. They call the cops at the first sign of trouble.

Guests at upscale hotels are *never* careful. Otherwise vigilant people are fooled by all that marble and gold leaf into thinking they're somehow safe from the unwashed 99 percent. It's practically an invitation, the way they leave their stuff unattended all over the place—in elevators and stairwells, in ballrooms and conference halls, on luggage carts "accidentally" abandoned by undertipped porters, on the pavement right next to their luxury rental cars, and sometimes just stacked up like so much designer firewood outside their rooms. It would be a crime *not* to swipe something.

I realize that might sound bad or wrong or whatever, but I've given this a lot of thought, and the conclusion I've reached is that "rightness" and "wrongness" are slippery concepts. I mean, some things are obviously shitty, and some things are obviously nice or noble or whatever, but between the two goalposts of black and white, between punching a baby in the kidney and donating a kidney to save a baby, there's a freaking football field's worth of gray area. (Side note: When I first learned about the Ten Commandments in Sunday school, I thought "covet" was another word for "have sex with," which made a lot of sense when it came to "Thou shalt not covet thy neighbor's wife," but a little bit less when it came to "Thou shalt not covet thy neighbor's animals," and not at all when it came to "Thou shalt not covet they neighbor's house." Turns out it just means "want to have." That's the problem with the Bible—or one of them, anyway—it doesn't just tell you what to *do*, it tells you what to *want*. That's too much to ask, IMHO.)

Take stealing, for example. My dad taught me that our society punishes people who only steal a *little*, but it rewards people who steal a *lot*. Like the assholes on Wall Street who make you take on all these crazy loans just to get a house or go to college, loans you have to pay back twenty times over with all the interest and shit. Or the assholes in all these countries that just happen to have oil or coal or trees or whatever, making huge profits off natural resources that ought to belong to the whole world. Or the assholes in Washington, DC, always coming up with some new law that taxes the kind of people who clean the toilets at the Palace Hotel more than the kind of people who stay there.

"Be careful," my dad used to say. "Pretty much anytime anyone opens his mouth, he's trying to take something from you."

So you tell me, with all these epic klepto atrocities going on behind the scenes, what difference does it make if I take a few bucks out of some high roller's pocket (or suitcase, or unlocked car)? In fact, isn't the kind of stealing *I* do about a million times better than the other kind of stealing? I'm like Robin Hood, really. I steal from the rich and give to the poor. Except in my case, the poor is me.

I glanced around the room, and when I was sure no one was looking, I reached over and undid the clasp of the silver-haired girl's little blue handbag. I pushed through a cloud of Kleenex and deep-sea dove into the mysterious mire of femininity until my fingers found the wad. A second later I was up on my feet and out of there.

THE RETURN OF THE JEDI

I'D STOLEN PLENTY OF STUFF IN MY LIFE, and I'd never felt even a little bit bad about it. But as I made my escape across the lobby of the Palace Hotel, riffling that thick stack of bills in my pocket, a huge foaming tsunami of guilt slammed into me. Maybe because it was more money than I'd ever seen at once in my entire life. Maybe because even though the girl was dressed like a rich girl, I couldn't have said for sure that she was rich, because actual rich people usually keep their cash in banks and bonds and shit, not in a messy wad at the bottom of their purses. Or maybe it was just because I knew there were a lot of ways to make money, but only one perfectly sad silver-haired girl sitting alone in the Palace Hotel.

And so I made the mistake of looking back.

When I was little, my parents would read me one fairy tale every night before bed, always from one of the volumes my dad kept over his desk: Grimm, Andersen, those Blue and Red Fairy Books. They wouldn't skip over the gross or scary stories, the ones with girls who chopped off their heels to fit into shoes, or vengeful demons, or tricksy Death. I couldn't believe it when I finally heard the weak-sauce, sanitized versions of these stories we got in school; a "Cinderella" without a bunch of blood-filled shoes is no "Cinderella" at all. And did you know that, in the original "Sleeping Beauty," there's no handsome prince who rouses Sleeping Beauty with a gentle kiss? Nope! It's actually a douche-bag king—one who already has a queen, by the way—and he *rapes* her. She wakes up pregnant, so the king's wife tries to kill her, bake her into a pie, and feed her to the king. The happy ending? The king decides to have his wife burned to death so he can raise a family with Sleeping Beauty. Make a friendly animated film out of *that* shit, Disney.

Anyway, my parents also read me the Greek myths, which tend to be about gods who come down from Olympus to get it on with hot chicks. My dad's favorite character was Orpheus, the famous musician who was allowed to bring his dead wife back from Hades, as long as he could make it to the surface without checking to see if she was actually behind him. But he peeked, and ended up losing her forever. I always thought Orpheus got kinda screwed there. I mean, would you trust the Lord of the Underworld not to mess with you? But my dad said it was the most perfect myth ever written, because it represented the most fundamental human error: we all look back.

When I did, I saw that the silver-haired girl had returned to her seat. In spite of the fact that her purse was open and half its contents had spilled out across the tablecloth, she wasn't screaming or crying or scrambling around, looking for the culprit. Why, you ask? Because she'd been distracted by something else. By what, you ask? Well, by my journal, of course! I'd left it behind when I tore off with all that money. It had my name in it, and my e-mail address, and an incredibly embarrassing story I'd recently written called "The Most Beautiful Girl in the Kingdom," which she was now reading.

STORY #1:
THE MOST BEAUTIFUL GIRL IN THE KINGDOM

ONCE UPON A TIME, IN THE LAND OF AGERASIA, there lived a young cooper and his wife. They'd only been married a few months, but the cooper's wife was already pregnant. The cooper hoped for a boy, who would be his apprentice and one day inherit the workshop. But when the happy day arrived, his wife gave birth to a bouncing baby girl with hair the color of sunlight. They called her Gilda.

"Well, anyone can make a mistake," the cooper said.

Soon after that, a second child was on the way. This time, the cooper was more insistent: "Woman, you absolutely must produce a boy for me." But his disobliging wife churned out yet another girl. This one had hair the color of copper in candlelight, and so she was called Cypria.

"Come now," the cooper said. "To give birth to one girl may be regarded as a misfortune. To give birth to two looks like carelessness." As punishment, he beat his wife around the belly with a bent piece of barrel wood.

Soon after that, she became pregnant for a third time. The cooper, though not a particularly devout man, spent all his free time at the village temple, begging the gods to finally grant him a son. But after only six months, his wife went into labor. For three days and three nights, she lay abed, panting like a bellows, only to produce a creature as tiny, wrinkly, and purple as a raisin, with a head of silver hair so fine it looked like a layer of dust. The cooper's wife took one look at the child, said simply "I'm sorry," and died.

The midwife was certain the baby girl wouldn't survive the night, so the cooper neglected to name her. Only the baby did survive the night, and the one after that, and the one after that, and then she began to put on weight and the midwife said the danger was past.

But the cooper still refused to give the girl a name. The truth was, he hated her, because she had survived where his wife had not, and now he would never have a son.

Years passed. Cypria and Gilda were happy, gregarious children, but their silver-haired sister, constantly beaten and berated by her father, forced to do all the most arduous household chores, grew cold and aloof. She didn't speak until she was five, and then it was only to ask her sisters to please shut up, because she was trying to think. Her hair grew long and lustrous, but it remained the same stubborn shade of silver. Behind her back, the townsfolk said that a demon had slipped into her body because her father hadn't given her a name. They would spit into the dirt after she walked past, a practice that was said to ward off evil spirits.

On the silver-haired girl's fourteenth birthday, the king of Agerasia died suddenly. Rumors had it that his son, the crown prince, was responsible. The prince had always hated his father for marrying him off to the princess of a nearby kingdom, a girl so fat that special thrones had to be built to accommodate her girth.

Not long after the prince became king, a book of humorous limericks began to circulate around Agerasia. It was called "The Spherical Monarch," and its sole subject was the queen's prodigious size (a sample verse: "There once was a lady so chubby/she couldn't fit into the tubby/she then became queen/but the wedding night scene/was a bloodbath, she crushed her poor hubby!"). When the king heard about the book, he was so angry that he immediately ordered his army to sweep the country for every girl between the ages of twelve and eighteen.

"If she be comely, cut her down where she stands," he said, "until my queen is the most beautiful girl in the kingdom."

The soldiers did as they were told, driving beauty before them like so much cattle to the slaughter. Before long, one of these soldiers came to the village where lived the cooper and his three daughters.

Hurriedly, the cooper dressed Gilda and Cypria in the clothes of his late wife and used a coal pencil to draw fine wrinkles on their faces. Then he sent them to their tiny rooms, which were windowless and dank and would hopefully mask their true ages.

The silver-haired girl didn't have her own room—she spent her nights on a straw-filled pallet in her father's workshop—so there was nowhere for her to hide. Nor did her father make the slightest effort to disguise her.

"Put on a pot of tea for the king's man," he said. "And be quick about it."

The girl did as she was told. A few minutes later, a young soldier burst into the house.

"Who lives here?" he asked.

"Just me and my elderly aunties," the cooper said.

"Is that so?"

The soldier threw open the door to Gilda's room. The girl sat in a rocking chair, darning a pair of socks, quivering with fear.

"Who are you?" the soldier barked.

"Just an old woman," Gilda said. But the soldier could hear the brightness of youth in her voice.

"Off with your bonnet," he said.

Gilda knew she'd be finished if the soldier saw her honeycomb of golden locks, so she leaped out of the chair, brandishing a knitting needle like a dagger. The soldier was ready, however, and he separated her head from her body with one clean swing.

He entered Cypria's room next.

"Who's there?" Cypria asked, pretending to have just awoken from a dotard's midday nap.

"A representative of your king," the soldier barked. "Who are you?"

"Just an old woman," Cypria said. But the soldier could hear the brightness of youth in her voice.

"Off with your bonnet!"

Cypria was a clever girl, and before going into her room, she'd dusted her whole head with flour. Unfortunately, she'd forgotten about her eyebrows, which glimmered like a couple of bronze ingots. A cloud of flour billowed up into the air when her severed head struck the floor.

The soldier returned to the kitchen, where he noticed the silver-haired girl, who was just then pouring the hot water for tea.

"And who are you?" he asked.

The girl didn't answer.

"She doesn't have a name," the cooper explained.

"Oh no? Take off your bonnet, woman."

The silver-haired girl did as she was told, unleashing the coruscant cascade of her platinum tresses. The soldier leaned in closer, checking her eyebrows and eyelashes, which were both appropriately hoary. Finally he looked into her eyes, and the sorrow he found there was as depthless and ancient as the sea.

Satisfied, he drew his sword and put it through the cooper's stomach. "You lied to me," he said. "You only have one elderly auntie."

"A cup of tea before you go?" the silver-haired girl asked.

She wasn't afraid that the soldier would hear the brightness of youth in her voice, because she had never really been young.

"No thank you, ma'am," the soldier said, and left.

The silver-haired girl buried her sisters and her father in the garden. She lived out the rest of her long life alone, as the most beautiful girl in the kingdom.

SIMPLE QUESTIONS

I'D GOTTEN ONE THING RIGHT IN MY STORY.
Up close, I could see the startling color of the silver-haired girl's eyes: greenish-gray, oceanic. Her heart-shaped mouth was pursed in a frown so compact it was almost a pucker. She looked up when she'd finished reading and didn't seem in the least surprised to see me sitting across from her.

"Platinum and silver aren't the same color," she said. "Platinum is whiter."

I placed the wad of bills on the table between us, then gestured for my journal.

"Are you suggesting a trade?" she asked, and there was something playful in her tone, almost as if she didn't care that I'd just robbed her. I nodded. She closed my journal and held it to her chest. "Thank you, but I'd rather have the story. I've always believed in supporting the arts."

Just then the waiter came back to the table.

"Sir, you left without paying for your coffee."

I smiled, because there was something ridiculous about getting in trouble for stealing five bucks' worth of coffee when I'd nearly walked off with a good five grand.

"Is that funny to you?" the waiter said.

Another great thing about hotels is that it's almost impossible to get in trouble inside one. Everyone assumes you're a guest, which means you're a tourist, which means you're probably an idiot. If someone catches you hanging around somewhere you're not supposed to be, all you have to do is put a look of utter confusion on your face, as if you just woke up in someone else's body. It's a little bit harder for me, given my condition, but I've learned how to roll with it. I get out the old notebook and write something like: *I am looking to the bathroom* or *Can you explain me how is the Golden Gate Bridge?* or that old classic *No hablo ingles*. I bet I could get caught in some rando's hotel room in the middle of the night, standing over the bed, wearing nothing but a Speedo and sharpening a butcher's knife, and probably get away with it.

The waiter, true to his profession, was still waiting for my answer.

As nonchalantly as I could, I peeled one of the bills off the stack, just like the girl had done a few minutes earlier, and offered it up. The waiter was momentarily torn between his desire to be pissed off and his desire to have another hundred bucks. He made the right call.

"This has been an expensive breakfast," the girl said, after the waiter had gone. I nudged the wad of cash toward her, but she nudged it right back.

"Not yet. I've got some questions for you. Was this story written about me?"

I shrugged.

"Yes or no?"

I shrugged again, finally earning a little scowl, which somehow made the girl even *more* pretty. It brought a bloom to her pale cheeks and made sharp shelves of her cheekbones. Shit but she was pretty.

"It's very rude not to answer simple questions," she said.

I gestured for my journal, but she still wouldn't give it to me, so I took out my pen and wrote *I can't* on my palm.

Then, in tiny letters just below it, I finished the thought: *Now don't you feel like a jerk?*

MY FIRST DATE
WITH DR. MILTON

DR. MILTON HAD A LARGE PHOTOGRAPH OF
a banana above his desk. He caught me staring at it when I first
sat down in his office. I was twelve years old.

"That was already there when I moved in," he said. "Maybe
the last person who worked here was a gorilla."

I liked him. He had a beard that went all the way around his
face, like a lion's mane, and he wore the same kind of glasses
my dad used to wear when he was working—thin black frames,
squared off at the corners.

"Parker, do you know what germs are?" he asked.

He had me write my answer on a wide yellow notepad with
a chunky red marker that smelled sweetly toxic. I still have that
pad somewhere in my room.

They make you sick, I wrote.

"That's right. Germs are little tiny things that get in your
body and make you sick. But there are ways to be sick that
don't involve germs because they don't involve your body. Your
mind can get sick."

Like when you're crazy.

Dr. Milton laughed a genuine laugh (by my estimation,

about 80 percent of all laughs are fake), which I appreciated. "Well, nobody's calling anyone crazy, Parker. But you do understand why your mom is worried, don't you?"

I did. It was because I'd refused to go to school ever since the accident six months before. Because I threw a silent tantrum anytime she suggested I leave the house, as if going outside were one and the same with the end of the world. Oh, right, and the whole "not speaking" thing.

Because I can't talk, I wrote.

"I'm not convinced yet that you can't talk. In fact, I'm going to try and convince you that you can. Would you like to play a game?"

Okay.

Dr. Milton took out a bunch of white cards with weird blobs on them; I learned later this was called a Rorschach test.

"What do you see here?" he asked.

I looked hard, trying to figure out what he wanted me to see. I was old enough to understand that this wasn't a game at all, but a test. *A teenage mutant ninja turtle standing on top of a bat,* I wrote; then, seeing the expectant look on Dr. Milton's face, added, *And a panda bear. With some sheep.*

"Do any of these animals scare you?"

No.

"Do they look like they're moving?"

No.

"What about this one?"

He held up a different card.

It's scary.

"It scares you?"

It looks like a sea monster.

He showed me more cards—another sea monster (this time with octopus arms), a bowlegged cowboy riding a donkey made of metal, a field of flowers—and then he went through the cards all over again. Then I had to arrange them in order of clearest image to least clear image.

"You like this, don't you?" Dr. Milton asked.

It's okay.

"You like being creative."

I guess.

"Do you want to write things, like your dad did?"

I shook my head.

"Why not?"

Dad wasn't happy.

"How do you know that?"

I thought about it for a while but couldn't come up with a good answer. I just knew. I think kids have a knack for detecting happiness, but they lose it as they get older. They have to. Otherwise they'd notice how unhappy everybody else is, and they'd never be able to be happy themselves.

I don't know.

"Are *you* happy, Parker?"

That was a tough question too. I glanced up at the banana, which curved upward at both ends, like a big yellow smile. It made me want to cry. So I cried.

Dr. Milton didn't give me a diagnosis that day. It would be a few more months before we'd start discussing my problems by their Christian names—complicated grief disorder, trauma-induced psychogenic aphonia, social anxiety. What he did give me was a project. He said that he thought that the reason I didn't want to leave the house was because I didn't want my life to go on without my dad there. He said I should start writing a journal, to keep track of all the things that happened to me during the day, as if I were writing letters to my dad. It seemed like a pretty stupid idea to me, but it worked. Within a couple of months, I stopped being afraid to leave the house. Another couple of months after that, and I was willing to go back to school. Of course, the journaling thing wasn't supposed to be a permanent fix—more like a brief stop on the transcontinental train ride back to mental health. Only my train never quite got moving again.

Dr. Milton said the only way to fix my speech disorder would be to see a specialized therapist, so he set me up with Dr. Joondeph. Dr. Joondeph gave me this exercise to do, where I would try to hum my way into a word, because humming is supposed to relax the vocal cords. He told me I could get better, but I would have to apply myself. It could take months, maybe even years, to recover.

I've kept seeing Dr. Milton—once a week for almost six

years now—but I refused to go back to Dr. Joondeph after that first session, and I only tried his exercise a handful of times.

Mom says that when I was a little kid, I liked to pick these red berries off a big bush in Golden Gate Park. Apparently, I could spend whole afternoons out there without talking to anyone, filling up a bucket with berries, carrying it over to the ivy to dump it out, and then starting all over again. She says my dad found the whole thing hilarious. "Our son's going to grow up to be a migrant worker!" he would say.

This was long before the accident, long before "psychogenic aphonia" became a part of my vocabulary, but I still preferred activities that didn't require a lot of conversation. They say that God gave us two ears and one mouth because listening is twice as important as talking. That makes a lot of sense to me. Of course, God also gave us two nostrils, one butthole, thirty-two teeth, and ten toes. So I'm not sure where that leaves us. All I know is that I've never really minded my disorder. Dr. Milton says I might even like it now, because it's become such a big part of who I am. And it *is* pretty great not to be expected to answer every idiotic question a teacher asks me, or laugh at every idiotic joke a classmate makes, or sing "The Star-Spangled Banner" at sporting events. Besides, it's not like I'm the only one with problems. Sometimes it seems like half the kids at school have some kind of ADD or ADHD or Asperger's or whatever. I think most of them are just a little stupid. I'm not stupid; I'm just dumb.

(That's a joke.)

COMPUTER GAMES AND INTERNET PORNOGRAPHY

"YOU CAN'T SPEAK?" THE SILVER-HAIRED
girl asked.

I shook my head.

"So you just write in this, I suppose." She flipped my journal
open to the first page: *Journal #105. Return to Parker Santé,
parkerofsherwood@gmail.com. Do not read. And yes, I realize
that probably only makes you want to read it more, but don't.
Seriously.*

"Does this mean you've filled out a hundred and four other
journals?"

I nodded, and I wondered if she could tell that I was
proud of that fact. Sure, I was a freak, but at least I was
a *super*-freak. And I loved the way they looked, all those
journals lined up on a single bookshelf in my room, carving a
path through time that you could follow, like a trail of bread
crumbs, from that first day in Dr. Milton's office right up to
the present. It was as if I'd archived myself inside them—my
own private horcruxes.

"I suppose you don't have much of a choice, do you?" the
girl said. "We all have things we need to get off our chests.

Most people just talk and talk until there's no one left to listen. You talk to your journals. It's practically poetic."

I have "Practically a Poet" printed on all my business cards, I wrote.

The girl smiled. It was the first time she'd done that, and for some reason it made me think of that smile-shaped banana painting in Dr. Milton's office, the one that had made me cry. "How old are you, Parker Santé?"

I held up ten fingers, then seven.

"Seventeen? What a horrible age. I bet you spend most of your free time playing computer games and watching pornography on the Internet."

People who can speak don't know this, but it's much harder to lie when you don't have access to words. The mind might be treacherous, but the body is a Boy Scout—it's always trying to give away your secrets. I put on an expression that I hoped conveyed offense and denial simultaneously. The girl didn't buy it for a second.

"Grubby little seventeen-year-old-boy hands. Disgusting."

Are you older than me?

"Time flows differently for girls," she said dismissively, then flagged down a passing waiter. "Garçon? Two more coffees, if you would, and make it snappy."

I gave her a funny look, because really, who said shit like that? It reminded me of this one time that Mr. Bear, my American history teacher, called a paper I'd written "anachronistic," which meant that it didn't correctly describe the time period it was supposed to (in his defense, I *had* written a fictional version of the Civil War that involved a lot of Confederate androids with laser muskets and almost no reading of the assigned textbooks). That word was a perfect fit for the silver-haired girl. She didn't seem like a normal teenager—more like something between a space alien and a homeschooled kid. Or maybe she was just a lot older than she looked. There was this girl in my chemistry class named Laura who was half Dutch and half Native American, and she had these hands that I swear could have belonged to an old woman: weather-beaten, tanned like old leather, crosshatched with wrinkles. Basically, a palm reader's wet dream. The silver-haired girl was a little like that, except instead of her hands seeming too old, it was her whole personality.

"So tell me, Parker Santé, what has inspired you to fill up a hundred and four and a half journals in your short and sordid seventeen years on this planet?"

I didn't usually answer that question honestly, but I wanted to throw something in the girl's way, something that might shake her seemingly unshakable composure.

I stopped talking after my dad died, I wrote, then prepared myself for the usual things people said after I told them that.

"What a remarkably asinine thing to do."

That was not the usual things.

"I'm sorry if that sounds rude, Parker, but I hardly see

what your father dying has to do with what sounds like—and you'll have to excuse me again if this comes across harshly—an almost deranged sort of graphomania. My father died, and I never wrote a single word about it."

My therapist said it might help, at least until my voice came back. But my voice never came back, because I wouldn't go to speech therapy.

"Why ever not?"

Before I could answer, the waiter returned with two fresh cups of coffee. The girl poured cream and dropped a big boulder of brown sugar into her cup. She went to do the same to mine, but I put my hand over it just in time.

"Really?" she said. "I've never understood people who take their coffee black. Isn't life already bitter enough?"

That's what I like about it. Life isn't sugarcoated. Why should coffee be?

"The first reasonable point you've made, Parker Santé. Cheers." We toasted coffee mugs. "But we were talking about your strange condition. You refuse to go to speech therapy, and instead you rob innocent strangers in hotels. Do I have that about right?"

Innocent people don't usually have fat stacks of hundreds in their purse.

"Then I am the exception that proves the rule. This money is everything I have left in the world."

For real?

The girl nodded.

Then you should probably put it in a bank or something.

"But I just took it out."

Why?

The girl stared at me for a few seconds, as if weighing her options. Then she opened up her purse and took out a cell phone. She placed it between us on the white tablecloth. "I am waiting for a phone call. And when it comes, I'm going to give this money to the first needy person I see. Then I'll take the trolley to the Golden Gate Bridge and jump off it."

Now I know what you're thinking. You're thinking that if someone said something like that to you, you'd just assume it was bullshit. And so would I. But you have to trust me when I tell you that the way the girl said it was *really* convincing. I mean, it didn't seem like a performance, or a cry for help, or a joke. She'd stated it as a simple, undeniable fact. So even if I didn't really believe that she would do it, I did believe that *she* believed she was going to do it.

The Palace Hotel's pretty far from the Golden Gate Bridge, I wrote. *Why wait here?*

"Because I met someone in this very room who became very important to me. His name was Nathaniel. I was working here as a waitress, and he asked me why I wasn't in school—" Suddenly the girl had a thought. "Wait a minute. Isn't it a school day?"

Finish your story. You were a waitress? How old are you?

33

"Answer my question, Parker."

Answer mine.

"I asked first."

Fine! I wrote, underlining the word to emphasize my annoyance. *Yes, it's a school day.*

"So why aren't you at school?"

I skipped out. I do it all the time. Then, in response to her horrified expression: *It's Halloween!*

"Halloween is not that kind of holiday, Parker Santé. And if you skip out all the time, how are you going to get into college?" There was a scolding tone to her voice I didn't appreciate, or even understand. What did she care if I skipped out on school? I was nothing and nobody to her.

I'm not. I've got a criminal record and shit grades. No college would want me. Besides, I'm kinda schooled out at this point.

"But that's ridiculous. That little fairy tale you wrote me was lovely. You should keep writing."

I rolled my eyes with such intensity that I ended up rolling my whole head.

"Hey!" She reached out and put her hand on my arm. I could feel my hairs stand up on end, and I hoped she couldn't tell. "I will not allow you to squander your life."

You don't even know me.

"So what?"

Well, I'll make you a deal. I'll go to college if you don't jump off the Golden Gate Bridge.

"That's not . . ." She took her hand away, leaving a cold patch on my arm. "It's not the same thing."

Why not?

"Because I've earned the right to be bitter."

So have I.

We stared at each other across the table. Somehow, a conversation that I'd felt had at least been flirting with flirtation had turned into something more serious.

"Young people feel things so deeply, don't they?" she said quietly, almost to herself. "Everything's happening for the first time."

I wasn't sure how to respond to that, but the girl started speaking again before I got the chance.

"All right, Parker Santé," she said. "I've come to a decision. You'll be my needy person."

What?

"You'll be my needy person. The recipient of my largesse."

It took me a second to figure out what she meant. *Hold up, you mean you're gonna give me all that money?*

"Not give. God knows what stupidity you'd spend it on. We'll spend it together."

All of it?

"Every last cent. And in exchange, you have to promise me you will apply to *and* attend college. Deal?"

She put out a hand to shake.

WHAT I KNOW ABOUT LOVE

LOVE IS A LITTLE BIT LIKE GENETICS—SURE, there's an element of chance in there, but when all is said and done, you're probably going to end up taking after your parents.

My mom and dad loved each other. I know that much. But that's probably the best you could say for them. They loved each other like the ocean loves the shoreline—eating away at it, little by little, day after day. They loved each other like the sunlight that makes the plants grow, then scorches the leaves and bakes the moisture from the earth. They loved each other like the seagulls love the bronze statue they're always shitting all over.

My dad moved to the States from Colombia back in the early nineties. He'd gotten this prestigious scholarship to study medicine at UC San Francisco, but he never finished his degree. Unbeknownst to his family back home, he'd started taking creative writing classes at California College of the Arts, and he eventually dropped out of medical school to pursue writing full-time. He spent three years on his first novel, a pulpy science-fiction adventure that sold enough copies to cover the cost of a used Toyota Tercel and get him a teaching gig at CCA. My mom was studying poetry and Spanish there. They met at a bar in the Mission. Two years later they were married, with a porky little newborn baby named Parker. All I can remember about them as a married couple is a perpetual hum of anxiety, the same kind you feel when the heroine of a horror movie is hanging around the haunted mansion for the first time, and you know some seriously bad shit is gonna go down before too long.

So I guess what I'm trying to say is that I basically learned fuck all about love from my parents.

I've learned even less from direct experience, for obvious reasons. It's tough to romance a girl when you can't speak. My dad won my mom over with Neruda. (I've got his copy of the love poems now, in both languages: *"Para que tú me oigas/mis palabras/se adelgazan a veces/como las huellas de las gaviotas en las playas."* So that you will hear me, my words sometimes grow thin as the tracks of the gulls on the beaches.) But reciting love poems is to writing them down as a box of chocolates is to a box of croutons; there's just no comparison.

So what could I possibly know about love? I definitely didn't think I was "in" it or anything; I'd only met this girl a few minutes ago. All I knew was that I'd told way bigger lies than the one I was about to tell for way less important reasons, and if the alternative to lying was never seeing her again, I would've promised to go to a hundred colleges.

I reached across the table and shook her hand.

"Good," she said. "That's settled. I'm Zelda, by the way." She put the wad of bills back in her purse and stood up. "Now shut that silly notebook, Parker. We're going to the mall."

FOREVER 21

LIKE MOST PEOPLE WITH A BRAIN, I'VE always hated malls. And it's not just the insane specificity of a shop called the Art of Shaving, or the inexplicable cost of the ass-ugly plaids for sale at Burberry (what kind of raving serial killer psychotic would drop nine hundred dollars on a scarf?), or the fact that the whole building stinks of whatever toxic waste goes into Cinnabons and Wetzel's Pretzels, or the soul-crushing volume of the music that gushes out of Abercrombie & Fitch like so much sonic sewage. No, it's the *people* that really get to me. It's the minimum-wage-powered sales staff, made up half of hormonal, sulky teenagers (like me) and half of embittered adults railroaded back into the workforce by the recession (like my mom). It's the crush of foul-smelling skater punks, bleached-blond cheerleaders, testosterone-addled jocks, happy couples (rarer than sushi), unhappy couples (common as a cold), bawling babies, and the shitty parents who never bother to pick them up out of their strollers.

Also, it's pretty much impossible to steal from people in a mall, because of all the cameras.

Zelda seemed to share my general contempt for mall culture,

but instead of being depressed by the crass consumerism and mindless conformity, she found the whole thing hilarious.

"Look at that one!" she said, pointing out a Lids store and laughing a condescending little twinkle of a laugh. "Is there nothing in there but baseball caps? My God, your generation really will buy anything with a logo on it." She turned around and found a group of punkers chomping down on McDonald's burgers. "And what about these kids here? All dolled up like rebels, but spending their money at the biggest multinational corporation in the world." She grabbed hold of my hand with a little-kid-at-Disneyland sort of excitement. "You have to treat me exactly like a teenager, okay?"

I nodded, though I didn't have the slightest idea what she meant. Wouldn't I be treating her like a teenager just by, you know, *being* a teenager? Or maybe I'd been right about the homeschool thing, and she'd never had the chance to experience normal kid stuff. Or what if it was even worse? What if she'd been raised in some kind of crazy religious cult? That would explain the silver hair *and* the fact that she registered about a 9.2 on the weirdo-Richter scale.

"So what should we do first?" she asked.

C-l-o, I spelled out in sign.

"A little more slowly, please."

In the cab on the way over from the Palace Hotel, I'd taught Zelda the alphabet signs, but only because she'd practically begged me to. Truth is, I've always kinda hated signing. My mom hired this private tutor named Tara back when I was in middle school. She was a partially deaf girl who dressed in long hemp skirts and had a mandala tattooed on her shoulder. She wasn't a bad teacher, but she'd taken it personally when I told her I didn't want to be part of the deaf community. I don't think she understood that I just didn't want to be part of *any* community.

C-l-o-t-h-e-s, I finished spelling out.

"Obviously," Zelda said. "But where?"

Clearly, she didn't realize she was asking this of a broke-ass straight boy who'd gotten dressed this morning by using the smell test (Armpit #1? Check. Armpit #2? Check minus. Eh, good enough); I had no idea what stores sold the nice clothes. But I didn't want to let her down, so I started walking as if I knew where I was going. Pretty much everybody else in the mall was an adult (not surprising, given that it was just past ten a.m. on a school day), so it was impossible to use the clientele to tell which stores were actually cool. Luckily, just when I was about to give up and pick one totally at random, Zelda spotted a sign and burst out laughing.

"That is too perfect! We absolutely must go there."

I nodded in a way that I hoped made it look like I'd been planning for us to end up here all along.

"Maybe I'll even pick out a few things for myself, while we're at it."

We wandered slowly from rack to rack. Zelda would push the hangers from right to left, as if she were flipping pages in a book. Every once in a while she'd pull something out and hold it up, then say something like, "Would this look good on me?" or "Isn't this ghastly?" I'd nod, or shake my head, or shrug—whatever it seemed she wanted to "hear." We wound our way through the entire women's department and on into menswear. Zelda took a blue button-down shirt off the rack and pressed it up against my chest, as if I were a paper doll.

"Hold on to this one," she said, handing me the hanger.

After I'd been laden down with more clothes than I actually owned, we went to the dressing rooms. I sat on the carpet outside while Zelda changed. Just below the edge of the door, I watched her dress fall around her ankles, and I wondered what she would do if I limboed myself in there with her. At the other end of the hallway, back in the actual store, a salesperson quickly glanced in at us, then just as quickly slipped away. Was he worried that we might be trying to steal something, or that we might be hooking up?

"What do you think?"

Zelda's shapely legs, made smooth and black by leggings, were just a few inches away from my face. They disappeared beneath a very short leather skirt.

S-h-o-r-t, I signed.

"Clothes are all about highlighting your assets, Parker. I've got no chest to speak of, so I have to draw attention to my legs. I usually don't go in for things that are quite so revealing, but I figure it's now or never."

Before long, it was my turn in the hot seat. I'd never played this game with anyone other than my mom before. When she and I went shopping together, I'd grudgingly pick out a couple of T-shirts or a pair of pants, she'd insist I get a smaller size, and then we'd call it a day. But Zelda wanted a show. I came out wearing a pair of tight black jeans that I'd had to hop around in like an idiot just to fit over my hips. She gestured for me to spin. I shook my head.

"Don't be silly, Parker. I have to see the fit. Jeans are all about the rear view." I gave a silent sigh, then turned around.

"That's your asset right there," she said.

I looked at myself in the three-way mirror. These jeans were a lot nicer than the ones I'd come in with. The old pair was balled up on the dressing room floor—a pale-blue pile of thready denim, so big that they fell off if I didn't wear a belt. The new ones were clean and straight-lined, more adult somehow. I looked taller in them, maybe even a little skinnier.

"Stop staring at yourself, you narcissist, and try on the shirt with the red collar."

We spent a good hour in that dressing room, though it only felt like a few minutes. It's weird, but some people are a lot better at talking to me than others. I can feel like I've had a conversation even when I haven't said a word. Dr. Milton says it's about the quality of someone's attention. Most of my teachers suck at it. My mom has good days and bad. But Zelda was a champion. She filled up the silences that might've been awkward, making fun of the other people who came into the store ("She needs a shop called Forever 51, am I right?"), chatting up the salespeople ("Why is everything here made in China? Whatever happened to American manufacturing?"), and asking me a lot of yes-or-no questions (the easiest to answer when you can't speak). I did notice that she hadn't told me anything about herself yet, but I could understand that. I was usually pretty slow to open up too. In fact, Zelda was the first person I'd talked about my dad with in . . . well . . . ever.

When we were finished trying things on, she carried our stack of clothes up to the register. The total was $614.23—a mind-demolishing amount of money, in my world—but Zelda just handed over seven of the hundred-dollar bills like they were a bit of loose change.

"You'll be a gentleman and carry the bags," she told me.

The hour we'd spent in Forever 21 was already more than enough shopping for me, but Zelda insisted we hit up a couple more stores. She bought me a pair of sunglasses with small perfect circles for lenses ("Just like Lennon," she said), this crazy watch that was made of wood and cost as much as all the Forever 21 clothes put together, and a few more shirts from a department store where even the mannequins looked rich.

After we'd finished shopping, we retired to the food court for a couple slices of greasy pizza.

"My God," Zelda said after her first bite. "It's every bit as deliciously disgusting as it looks."

You act like you've never eaten mall pizza before, I wrote in my journal.

"I've been abroad for the past few years. Not much chance to visit malls."

Abroad? For real?

"For real," Zelda confirmed.

All right, I wrote. *Be serious with me. Where'd you get all this money?*

Zelda feigned shock. "Are you asking me about my finances? How gauche. I refuse to discuss such things sober." She took a small leather flask out of her purse and poured some of it into her soda. "Coke without rum is like toast without butter—utterly pointless." She mixed the cocktail around with her straw. "And to answer your question, I am neither rich nor not rich. And the point is moot now anyway."

Why?

"You know why."

It took me a second to figure out what she meant.

Because you're going to jump off the Golden Gate Bridge when that phone call comes in.

"Bingo."

But you agreed not to do that if I applied to college.

"Those were not the terms of our agreement, Parker Santé." She sipped at her drink, smiling mischievously, and I realized she was right. The deal we'd ended up shaking on wasn't "I apply to college; you don't jump." It was "You spend all your money; I apply to college." Zelda had taken the whole Golden Gate nosedive thing off the table without my even noticing. And though I still didn't think she'd actually do it, I didn't appreciate being tricked. I'd have to keep a close eye on the cash from here on out. By the terms of the deal, she couldn't disappear on me until we'd spent all the money ("Every cent," as she'd put it), and I was going to make sure we never did.

"So tell me, Parker, what do you and your friends do next, after you go shopping?"

I don't have friends. And if I did, we wouldn't go shopping.

"You don't have friends? Don't be silly. Everyone has friends."

Not really. There are kids I talk to at school, but no one I actually hang out with.

"Then I suppose you'll have to pretend. Imagine you're the most popular kid in your whole class, all right? You have friends and girlfriends galore. A jam-packed social calendar. Now, what would you and your vast coterie do after a morning of retail therapy? Remember, I'm looking for the authentic teenage experience here."

Once again, I had no idea how to answer Zelda's question, because I wasn't really living the authentic teenage experience. But then I realized it didn't matter how I answered, because if she really was this clueless, she wouldn't know if I was right anyway. I could've told her that after a few hours of shopping, most kids liked playing laser tag, or spray-painting the insides of churches, or freestyle walking at the nearest retirement home. So I decided to go with the most romantic thing I could think to do in the middle of the day at a mall.

M-o-v-i-e, I finger spelled.

Zelda's face lit up. "Of course! Something frightfully bad, I hope. About superheroes, maybe, or young idiots falling in love." She clapped her hands together in joyful anticipation. "Perfect! Let's do that!"

I knew she meant *Let's go see a movie*, but a part of me heard it differently, as if what she'd really meant was *Let's go fall in love*.

WHAT YOU DO
AT A MOVIE THEATER

YOU SIT IN THE BACK ROW. THE NEAREST other people are two rows away: an elderly couple who will spend the entire movie slowly unwrapping hard candies. You have a large bag of popcorn so drenched in butter it smells a little like paint thinner. You have big waxy red cups full of rum and Coke. Your arm rests at your side, not daring to step up to the actual armrest, which is a fraught location not unlike the no-man's-land that existed between the trenches during World War I. This is the first time you've ever been alone in a movie theater with a girl—a critical adolescent milestone, you are well aware—and you're terrified of screwing it up. When you reach for a particularly juicy kernel of popcorn and find a couple of greasy fingers waiting for you, you pull away so fast she asks if you're okay. But eventually, you let your elbow creep onto the back portion of the armrest, where it meets another elbow. You wonder if she knows that she is touching your elbow, because it might be that she just hasn't noticed yet, and the film has started now and it's sorta funny, so it's always possible that she's just not focused on her elbow at the moment. (Because how often are we ever really focused on the sensations in our elbows?) So you move your arm just a little bit—"I'm here!" your elbow announces—but she doesn't move, which means she must know that your elbow is there, and more importantly, that it is touching her elbow. Of course, you aren't sure if elbow contact really has any meaning, romantically speaking. Elbow contact could be a form of friend contact, like the way athletes are always smacking each other's asses, or the way the drama kids at school are always giving each other back massages on the steps in front of the theater. But fortune favors the bold and all that shit, so after twenty minutes or so, you put your whole arm up on the plush pillow of the armrest and let it lie against her arm. There's no denying this, then. It's skin against skin. Only a moment later, she moves her arm off the armrest, and the whole world begins to collapse like an imploded building, except then she picks up the tub of popcorn and puts it on the floor, raises the armrest, and nestles herself into your side. There is no hesitation or doubt in her movements, and you wonder how it is she manages to do everything this way, with such extreme confidence. She stays there for the rest of the movie, so close that you're afraid you'll dislodge her if you breathe too heavily. Then, as the credits begin to roll, she tilts her head toward you, and you feel her hot breath on your neck, and you think how strange it is that the body runs at 98.6 degrees, day and night, summer and winter, hotter than the city of San Francisco ever gets, the kind of heat that makes people want to take off their clothes and jump in the ocean.

"Take me to a party," she whispers.

You don't want to move to get your journal, so you can only stare at her, waiting for elaboration. For the first time, you notice that she smells a little like almonds.

"It's Friday. Halloween, even. My phone hasn't rung yet. I want a big party. Can you find me one?"

You nod, because how could you say no to her now? She nestles back into your shoulder.

"Marvelous."

And that's what you do at a movie theater.

KILLING TIME, PART 1 (SCHOOL)

I'VE ALWAYS HATED SCHOOL. I KNOW THAT'S a cliché, and probably a really stupid thing to tell *you*, of all people, but it's the truth. I mean, what's not to hate? I have to get on a bus at an hour of the day that shouldn't even be allowed to exist, barely able to put one foot in front of the other, and I'm just waking up by the time it's all over. Between these bookends, a bunch of adults try to get me excited about the things they can only vaguely remember being excited about themselves, and that was years before they were hired to teach those things to roomfuls of kids who were unlikely ever to get excited about them. The only thing I really enjoy is this after-school elective I take called Chess & War, in which we read about chess, read about war, then play chess. Probably the best thing about it is how nobody there cares that I don't speak. See, usually, people who don't speak are considered rude. But if someone tries to talk to you while you're reading, or while you're thinking over a chess move, *they're* the one being rude. I am the least rude person in Chess & War.

After Zelda and I got out of the movie, I told her I'd have to go back to school if I was going to find her a party. She called a car, and we made it to campus just a few minutes into the last class period of the day.

"Here's my number," she said, keying it into my phone. "Text me the details when you have them."

What if your dreaded call comes in before then? I wrote.

She shut the cover of my journal before I could write anything else. "Then you'll just have to go without me."

I got my collection of shopping bags out of the trunk, then stood in the drop-off as the car drove away. Though I'd implied to Zelda that it would be a piece of cake to secure a last-minute Halloween party, I wasn't very confident about my chances. Truth is, I'm not exactly the partying type, and it's not just because I don't speak. Even before the accident, I preferred spending time on my own. I think I got that from my dad. He was a crazy-hard worker; when he wasn't teaching classes or grading papers, he was in his office, trying to write. My mom called him an absentee father, which was sort of a joke, because technically he was home all the time. But in another way, it wasn't a joke at all, because even when he was around, he wasn't really there, if you know what I mean. I think maybe he liked the worlds in his head better than the real one. As far as I ever knew, he didn't have any close friends, and his whole family (other than us) was back in Colombia. Once, when I was about nine or ten, I told him I wasn't very popular at school. He told me that friends were overrated, because the only person you could ever really count on was yourself. Weirdly, that answer actually made me feel better.

My point is that I learned how to be antisocial at a young age, and that tendency only got worse after I stopped talking. Oh, and then I think I freaked out a lot of people when I got in this big fight in eighth grade and a kid almost ended up dead. (It's not nearly as exciting as it sounds, but I'm gonna hold off on giving you the details just yet. You're still getting to know me, and I'd rather not totally poison you against me this early in the game.)

The result of all of this was that, at the time I met Zelda, I really didn't get out very much. Sure, over the years, I'd been invited to a few Christmas parties and bar mitzvahs and *quinceañeras*—always the kind of semipublic events where the guest list was about as selective as the hiring process at a KFC— but I almost never went. I knew that nobody really wanted me there, standing around, silent as a monolith, reminding everyone of death and sadness and mental illness. If I was compelled to go (i.e., when my mom got teary-eyed and melodramatic about my "self-imposed isolation"), all I did was stand in the corner and kill time with some cell phone game until I felt I could leave without seeming rude or weird. (Side note: I've always liked that phrase, "kill time." As if time were some kind of evil dragon that needed to be slain. Unfortunately, like everything else in the world, time dies of natural causes, year by year, hour by hour, second by second. It's a veritable time *massacre* going on out here.) Dances, I quickly learned, are particularly bad for the speechless. The only way I could ask someone to slow dance involved a whole humiliating mime act. And if you weren't going to slow dance, there was really no reason to go to a dance at all; everyone knew that the fast songs were only there so you could scope out the geography and choose a target for when the slow jam dropped.

Still, in spite of my utter lack of popularity or plausible social contacts, I would have to make an effort. If I didn't find a party, I'd probably never see Zelda again, and that thought was enough to make *me* want to jump off the Golden Gate Bridge.

I waited out eighth period and then went to the only plausible party-reconnaissance venue I had: Chess & War.

As Mr. Tower began to describe the best responses to the Queen's Gambit, I cased the room as if it were a chessboard. As always, there were plenty of pawns—the dorkiest kids from the freshman and sophomore classes, happy to have found a place where they could spend forty-five minutes at a stretch without getting shoved or slammed or dissed. Obviously, they were useless to me. Then there were Danny Wu and Gabrielle Okimoto, the king and queen of the room, who co-captained the chess team and had been responsible for making Chess & War happen. Though they were gods in here, their influence didn't stretch far beyond the doors, and the only parties they got invited to involved dressing up like characters from the Lord of the Rings. No, what I needed here was a knight—the rare kid capable of jumping the border between the cool and the not-so-cool.

Such a creature did in fact exist, in the form of Alana Rodriguez. Alana was one of those people who had banked up enough social cred by being cute that she could get away with doing dorky shit in her free time. It didn't hurt that her boyfriend was Tyler Siegel, who fronted the only high school band that anybody cared about (they were called Möbius Stripper). He'd drop her off at Chess & War sometimes—kissing her just outside the door in a full-on, this-is-my-woman sort of way that you couldn't help but watch—then make some crack like "Hope you don't find yourself a better boyfriend in there." It was insulting, but also fair enough.

Alana and I weren't exactly tight, but we did have something of a bond, being the only Latino kids in the room. She was a few moves away from checkmate when I sat down next to her and a sweaty, aggravated Brian Suchland.

"You want next, Santé?" she asked.

I nodded.

"All right. Just let me finish wasting this bitch."

"Hey," Brian said, "I've still got a chance."

"A chance at getting wasted like a *bitch*," Alana said.

Though he was only down a pawn, Brian had totally lost control of the board. His bishops were blocked, one of his knights was still undeveloped, and his queen was stuck protecting his king. They were playing timed, of course, but Alana almost never gave more than a few seconds' thought to her moves. Her clock still had a minute and a half left on it when Brian finally conceded.

"Good game," he said, putting out a hand.

Alana didn't take it. "No, it wasn't," she said. Then, as he was walking away, "*Pinche baboso.*"

"What?" Brian asked.

"Nothing." She smiled sweetly.

I sat down in his still-warm seat.

"Does it smell like losing over there?" Alana said. "I bet it does."

I need to ask you a favor, I wrote, then spun my journal around so she could read it.

"Yeah? Is it not to wreck your face at this game we're about to play? Because the answer is no. I am most definitely going to wreck your face at this game we're about to play." Suddenly she reached out and grabbed hold of my wrist, pulling it up toward her face. "Hold up, P-Funk. Is this what I think it is?"

She was staring intently at the watch Zelda had just bought me. I nodded.

"I know what these things cost." She dropped my wrist and pointed at the little pileup of shopping bags just inside the classroom door. "Those are yours too?"

I nodded again.

"So what, you went on a shopping spree in the middle of the day?"

Sorta, I wrote.

"Damn, Santé. Are you Jay-Z or something?"

It's complicated.

She let out a long whistle as she began to set up the board. "And now, after a hard day of spending money, the big man wants a favor."

I need a party to go to. Tonight, if it's possible.

"That's interesting, see, 'cause I didn't know you went in for that kind of thing. You always seemed more the lone wolf type." She put her rook down, held it there a second, then lifted it up again and pointed it at me like a switchblade. "There's a girl involved, isn't there?" I shook my head. "A guy, then?" I shook my head again, more emphatically. "So it's a girl. Nice one, Santé!" She reached out for a fist bump, but when I went to bump her back, she slapped the back of my hand hard enough to sting. "But I'm not bringing you anywhere unless you beat me at this game. That's called stakes. I'll even let you go first."

But I'm black.

"You're Latino is what you are, son. And that whole white-goes-first bullshit is straight-up *racist*. Now hurry up and make your move. I'm only putting three minutes up."

I opened e4, and Alana went Sicilian—her favorite response. She also kept up a nearly nonstop monologue as we played. "They say that at, like, the highest levels, white wins about fifty-six percent of the time. Can you believe that shit? I mean, we're looking at a world where white folks win, like, ninety-five percent of the time. At least in chess, we could create a more equitable situation, you know what I'm saying?" Both of my knights were out now, putting their symmetrical pressure on the center of the board. "And what about gender distribution? How many of the pieces up in here are women? I don't even know what kind of genitals a rook's rocking, but knights are definitely dudes.

Bishops? Dudes. The king? Dude. Pawns could go either way, I guess, though they sorta look like little dicks. All we ladies have for sure is the queen." Bishops were developed. Kings castled. Alana went right on talking. "Now, I know what you're thinking: The queen's the most powerful thing on this board, right? But you see, that's even worse, because men are always putting us ladies on a pedestal. A woman can't just be a person, can she? We gotta be some kind of superhero or else we're nothing at all. Oh, you wanna play it like that?" I'd taken her queen; she took mine back. "See? That's what I'm saying. First chance you get, you're taking the only woman off the board. Look at this sausage party we got going on here now. It's like a boys' locker room up in this piece." We traded knights and a pawn. Things were still pretty even in terms of material, but I could feel Alana building up momentum. "Speaking of which, you know what I've always thought was weird? Checkers. Because anytime you make it to the other end of the board, you say 'king me'—'cause God knows you couldn't say 'queen me,' right?—and that means you put another dude on top of your dude. That's some weird sauce right there. Oh no, P-Funk, you should *not* have done that." She was right; I'd let my king and bishop get forked. "So here's a question for you: Is it harder to lose to a girl than a guy? Do you feel emasculated by my absolute dominance of these sixty-four squares? It's okay if you do, by the way. I probably would too." I was on the run now, my pawn structure in utter disarray. Finally I knocked my king over. Alana threw her hands up in the air.

"Victory! Mmm, yeah. It tastes so *good*! It's like filet mignon." She licked the tips of her fingers.

Thanks for the game, I wrote, and stood up.

"Hey, hey! Hold up there, Peebles. I was just messing with you. Of course I'll help with your lady. I've already humiliated you once today. I'm not a monster. Sit your crushed ass back down in that seat."

I did.

"You need a party."

I nodded.

"Well, that's easy. Jamie Schmid's doing his yearly Halloween bash tonight. Starts at nine. BYO shit."

I didn't know Jamie that well, but what I knew about him, I didn't like.

He wouldn't want me there, I wrote.

"Fuck that. I'll make sure it's cool. I got him wrapped around my little finger. Give me your number and I'll text you the address."

Thanks.

"My pleasure."

I stood up again, still a little amazed it had been that easy.

"Hey, Parker," Alana said. "It's good to talk to you. You should make a habit out of it."

I'd put my journal away, so all I could do was shrug.

KILLING TIME,
PART 2 (HOME)

I SKIPPED THE BUS SO I COULD RUN SOME important party-based errands on the way home. First I took the trolley downtown to this Halloween superstore thing that goes up every year for about two weeks. The place was packed with other last-minuters like myself, getting themselves outfitted for a night as Harry Potter or Katniss Everdeen or a slutty pharmacist or whatever. I'd come up with my own concept on the way over; I wanted something that would allow me to wear some of the clothes that Zelda had bought me that morning, but would still count as a costume. It only cost me about twenty bucks to get what I needed.

After texting Zelda the party info I'd gotten from Alana, I stopped at the Whole Foods near my house. They keep all their flowers right next to the front door, which is basically a giveaway. I had a hard time deciding; roses seemed like a fat red cliché, but most of the other flowers were ass ugly. Finally I just grabbed a handful of thick-stemmed sunflowers and walked out with them. The whole way home, I could see people staring at me, trying to figure out what the hell costume involved a normally dressed kid holding a bouquet of sunflowers in one hand and a bunch of shopping bags in the other.

We live in the Outer Sunset, a neighborhood at the far western edge of San Francisco. Our house has been in my mom's family for decades, but we didn't move there until after my dad died, because the place sorta sucks. It's basically the exact opposite of Doctor Who's TARDIS: way smaller on the inside than it looks on the outside. Claustrophobia sets in the second you walk through the front door. The kitchen is just a narrow alley between two counters. The oven door can't even open all the way; it sticks at an eighty-one-degree angle against the cabinets on the other side of the room (I measured it precisely with a protractor for a geometry assignment, for which I received a C–). There's no dining room, so we eat all our meals at the glass coffee table in the living room. A narrow set of stairs, each one a little bit higher than stairs are supposed to be, leads to the second floor, where my mom's bedroom and the house's one bathroom are. From the second-floor hallway, you grab a ring in the ceiling to pull down the ladder to the attic, where my room is.

"There's a frozen pizza in the oven," my mom said when I came in.

I spun the dial to 425. My mom was sitting on the living room couch, watching some random cop show, so she hadn't noticed all my bags. This might sound like a lucky break—it would be tough to explain how I'd ended up with thousands of dollars' worth of new clothes without stealing them—but the truth is, whenever my mom wasn't at work, the odds were pretty good she'd be sitting on that couch, watching TV. I quickly ran up to my room to drop off the bags, then came back downstairs. The eviscerated remains of a TV dinner were still in my mom's lap, and she was holding a mostly empty glass of red wine.

"Where've you been?" she asked. It wasn't an accusation, just a way to make conversation during a commercial break. She never really paid much attention to where I went or what I did.

Around, I signed.

"I love it there. Great appetizers. Hey, would you get a girl a refill?" I brought the bottle of wine in from the kitchen. When she turned around to take it, she noticed the bouquet of sunflowers I'd left on the counter.

"What are those?"

I'm going to a party tonight.

My mom did a double take. Then a triple take. Then a quadruple take.

Stop that.

"I'm sorry. But, I mean, this is voluntary? You haven't joined a cult? You haven't been brainwashed or hypnotized or anything?"

I don't think so.

"And the flowers, then . . . must be for a girl." Her face lit up. I shook my head, but it was too late. My mom was clearly a little bit tipsy, and this would've been exciting news anyway. "They are! They're for a girly girlity girl! A *bonita señorita*!"

Shut up.

"Okay. I'll zip it." But she was still smiling in that infuriating parental way, like she was in on a secret shared between her and all other adults ever. "Just tell me her name."

No.

"Is it Bonita the Señorita?"

Shut up.

"Fine, fine, fine."

Her show came back on, and we watched it together. Then we watched another one while I ate dinner. It was only a little after seven when I finished, but my mom had already passed out. She was slack-jawed and drooling on a couch cushion— the perfect candidate for a malicious Instagram post—but I wasn't that mean.

My mom had been a pretty woman when she was younger. I'd seen photos of her as a long-legged, almost ditzy-looking teenager, throwing her hair back in convertibles and posing lazily on beaches, wearing outfits that made my skin crawl (thinking of your parents being young is like thinking of Winnie-the-Pooh going to the bathroom: just fucking *weird*). But the past few years had been rough on her. After my dad died, she'd had to get a full-time job. There'd been life insurance, but after replacing the car and paying off my hospital bills and flying family members out from Colombia for the funeral, the money that was left over turned out to be just enough for a couple of movie tickets and a medium popcorn. She'd always liked traveling, so she trained to be a flight attendant for Delta. Turned out it wasn't as glamorous as she'd expected. The pay was shit, and her seniority was terrible, so she ended up getting saddled with tons of all-nighters. Then there were all the hours she had to spend on her feet, the obnoxious passengers, the restless nights in cheap airport hotels, the crap airplane food, the bone-dry air that she blamed for her expanding LTE network of crow's-feet.

She'd been away since the previous morning on a layover in Dallas. Of course she was fried. I gave her shoulder a squeeze. Her eyes were unfocused, blurry with fatigue and at least half a bottle of wine.

"Marco?" she said.

I shook my head, waited for her to recognize me as her son. But her eyes were filling up with tears now. "I was having a dream about you."

I'm not him, I signed.

"You were right over there," she said, pointing at the other end of the couch. "We were watching *The Simpsons* together." She wiped at the sticky corners of her mouth with the back of her hand, then at her wet cheeks. "It was so real," she said, and I could tell she'd finally phased back to reality.

I know.

She moaned a little bit when she stood up, took my arm like an invalid. I led her upstairs and put her in bed.

"Good night, Parky."

Good night.

I went up to my bedroom to get dressed. It took me a good half hour to choose my outfit; I hadn't quite realized just how much stuff Zelda had bought me. Finally I settled on the shirt with the red collar, a gray jacket, and the one pair of jeans that I could get into without contortions. Then I added the two props that turned the whole thing into a costume: a silver wig and a little orange-brown tail tufted with white. (Get it? No? Well, you have a few minutes here to try to work it out.) I didn't have a mirror in my bedroom, so I could only hope I looked presentable.

Back downstairs, I picked the sunflowers up off the kitchen counter, stole a bottle of wine from the rack, then headed out to the first party I'd ever given a shit about.

Zelda still hadn't responded to my text.

AN EVENING IN EIGHT DRINKS: INTRODUCTION

IT MIGHT SEEM WEIRD TO HATE PARTIES. Who hates parties? It's just a bunch of people getting together to have a good time, right? Wrong. It's a bunch of people getting together to be drunk, loud assholes, with a special emphasis on the *loud*. And another emphasis on the *drunk*. And a third emphasis on *assholes*, while we're at it.

Jamie lived just off Irving Street in the Inner Sunset, a twenty-minute walk from my place. The streets were overrun with a midget army of ghosts, witches, zombies, and Pokémon. It was a perfect Halloween night—thick with a fog that captured light and held it close, turning each streetlamp into a firefly cupped in the palms. The houses in the Sunset were closely spaced, laid out in colorful candy-button rows all the way down to the ocean. They were decorated with cobwebs and cardboard witches, tissue-paper ghosts and antique brooms. Every now and again you heard a little kid scream with pleasure-fear. I felt a brief burst of nostalgia for a time when a whole night spent collecting three bucks' worth of shitty candy was something worth looking forward to.

The party was audible from a couple of blocks away. Raucous

hip-hop beats clashed with the "spooky" ghost noises coming out of cheap boom-box speakers at nearby houses. As I was walking up the steps to Jamie's front door, a couple of young trick-or-treaters rushed past me, only to be called harshly back to the street by their parents, who recognized that this was not the place to go for a Kit Kat bar; true to form, Erik Jones was already vomiting into a pile of tiny white pumpkins artfully arranged on Jamie's stoop.

I dropped the bottle of wine off in the kitchen, then did a lap around the house looking for Zelda, but she was nowhere to be found. Out in the backyard, Alana was standing next to the keg, filling up cups for a couple of standard-issue vampires. She was dressed like a pirate, but she'd stuffed the back of her loose white pants with pillows. I got the joke right away, because it was even dumber than mine: Pirate's Booty.

"Look who made it out of the house," she said.

"Is that who I think it is?" Jamie Schmid, the host of the party, came running from the other end of the yard, a bottle of Budweiser gripped tightly in each fist. He was dressed like the bad guy from *The Karate Kid*, with COBRA KAI stitched onto his *gi*. He bore more than a passing resemblance to that guy, actually—reddish-blond hair, a pale face peppered with a few misleadingly wholesome freckles, and a palpable cruelty around the mouth, which rarely tautened into a smile as a result of anything other than its own jokes. "Fucking Charlie Chaplin has come to *my* party. I'm honored. And let me get a look at this costume." He grabbed me by the shoulders and spun me around like a doll. (I haven't mentioned this yet, but sometimes people treat me like a piece of furniture because I don't speak.) "You're a bunny rabbit, but with a bunch of dumb flowers. Peter Rabbit, right? Or Roger Rabbit?"

"He's a silver fox," Alana said, as if it were obvious.

"Ho!" Jamie put a hand over his mouth like some kind of MC. "That is the *shit*, Charlie. I love that. You just earned yourself a beer." He handed one of the bottles over.

"So where's this girl of yours?" Alana asked.

"She must not have gotten here yet," Jamie said. "I don't hear any oinking." He laughed.

"Shut up, Jamie." Alana lifted her beer in my direction. "Here's to you, Parker."

Unlike most kids I know, I've never seen the appeal in getting hammered every time there's alcohol on offer. But here I was at a party made up entirely of people I either didn't know or didn't like, so what else was I supposed to do? Down the hatch.

DRINK #1:
A BOTTLE OF BUD

I HADN'T BROUGHT MY JOURNAL TO THE party, because I didn't want to carry it around with me all night. I could see the pity in people's eyes when they watched me write. It's the one thing I can say for the Jamie Schmids of the world: their honest contempt is a million times easier to deal with than the stilted, stuttery sympathy that a lot of so-called "nice" people end up spewing. I'd much rather be treated like a freak than a charity case. Anyway, carrying my journal with me implied that I *wanted* to communicate but couldn't, when really I didn't mind keeping quiet. I wasn't here to make friends, as reality TV stars liked to put it. I was here for Zelda.

I stood in a classic awkward party circle with Alana, her boyfriend Tyler, Jamie, and three or four of Jamie's friends that I knew tangentially from school. They were talking about teachers, impersonating some and hating on some and admitting to crushes on others. Then they moved on to the stupidest answer any of them had ever given in class.

"Hey, Jamie," Tyler said, "you remember that time you said the third president was *almost* George Washington?"

"I stand by it. I was only off by, like, two presidents. That oughta be worth partial credit."

"There's no partial credit with hard facts," Alana said.

"Whatever. And you should talk, Tyler. You once said that the White House was the capital of America."

"I was eleven years old."

"You were stupid years old is what you were."

I was careful not to laugh. My laughter, I've been told, is a strange sight to behold—like a silent seizure. I just smiled, then plugged my mouth with the already empty bottle of Bud.

DRINK #2:
ANOTHER BOTTLE OF BUD

THE CIRCLE DISBANDED AS EVERYONE went to get another drink, and I was forced to engage in my least favorite party activity—wandering around pretending that I knew where I was going. I found the kitchen, where I grabbed another beer from the fridge and ate some Doritos. In the living room, I watched the DJ do that weird thing DJs do, where they hold one headphone to their ear and pretend that they're engaged in a really difficult and serious artistic task. I bounced my head to the beat for a minute, then headed deeper into the house to get away from the crowd. A closed door beckoned—Jamie's parents' room. It was funny: you could tell who slept where by the contents of the bedside tables. The one on the left featured a stack of books about World War II and a pair of nail clippers big enough to trim hedges with. The one on the right had a crystal ashtray with a lipstick-stained cigarette butt and a slim self-help book: *Finding Your Inner Goddess*.

Jamie's room was right next door. An unmade bed. A stack of *Maxim* magazines. A smell like the inside of a dirty mind, made up of equal parts Axe body spray and tube sock. The idiot had left his PS Vita plugged into the wall in plain sight. I slipped it into the inside pocket of my jacket.

Back in the hallway, Rosie Cuevas (dressed as a pink bunny) stood against the wall, waiting for the bathroom. She was checking her cell phone in that way you check your cell phone at a party, reading over your old text messages just to have something to do. Rosie was my first and only kiss, way back in the seventh grade, during a game of spin the bottle I'd somehow gotten involved in behind the library after a dance. The bottle had landed on her first, then on me, then *blam!* I was kissed. Kisses are weird that way. They're supposed to be performed by two people simultaneously, but they don't have to be. We even have a term for it—*a stolen kiss*—which is really just a euphemism for full-on oral assault. I can remember looking up from the open mouth of the bottle only to find another open mouth rushing at me. A crush of lip and tongue and saliva and the chorus of yowls from the onlookers. The next day I left a note in her school mailbox asking if she wanted to be my girlfriend. She politely declined.

"Parker!" she said, eyes lighting up in a way that was too sudden to be insincere. I raised a hand to say hey, but she bypassed it for a hug. "What the hell, man? You never come to parties!"

I shrugged.

"Hey, check this out. I still remember how to say 'I love you.'" She signed the phrase. "Was that right?"

I nodded. I'd forgotten that I'd taught her that.

"So have you started looking at applications yet? State wants all these essays and recommendations and stuff. It's nuts. I sorta thought you could just ask to be admitted and they'd say yes or no. Stupid, right?" The bathroom door opened and disgorged some kind of goth death fairy. "Anyway, wait for me out here, yeah? We should totally catch up."

But while Rosie was in the bathroom, a cheer came from the direction of the living room. It could've been anything—somebody taking off an article of clothing, somebody punching somebody else in the face, somebody beer bonging a forty of Olde English—but somehow I knew it was Zelda. I realized I was suddenly grinning like an asshole, so I took a moment to calm myself down.

Be cool, I signed to myself.

When I was sure I looked appropriately unenthusiastic, I headed for the living room.

DRINK #3:
A GLASS OF BUBBLY

THEY WERE CARRYING THEM FROM THE TRUNK of a limousine double-parked outside, straight through the house, and out onto the back deck: bottle after bottle of champagne. Zelda followed behind them, directing their labor. She was dressed like some kind of old-timey movie star, in a black dress with a neckline that plunged like a bungee jumper down her front, revealing two half scoops of vanilla skin on either side. Her hair had been smoothed into a tight wave and covered over with something halfway between a tiara and a hairnet, dripping black jewels down her forehead. Her eyes were ringed with mascara. I hardly recognized her, but in a good way.

"There you are, darling," she said to me, and her voice had an unfamiliar twinge of a Southern accent; apparently, it came with the costume. "I'm afraid I've become rather popular already, perhaps because I come bearing libations." Most of the partygoers were moving out to the back patio, following this fresh infusion of alcohol. "And what about you, Mr. Santé? Aren't you pleased to see me?" She slipped into my arms and kissed me on the cheek. The thousand tiny question marks of her hair tickled my neck. "Can you guess who I am?"

I didn't have the slightest idea, but I was saved by the sound of a cork popping out on the patio. "Heresy!" Zelda shouted. "Are they starting without me?"

She took my hand and led me outside. Jamie had already filled a red plastic cup with champagne, but when he saw Zelda, he sheepishly offered it up to her. She looked at it as if it were a dead mouse a cat had left on the doorstep.

"This is champagne, not Coca-Cola. Fetch glasses." Jamie laughed, but Zelda didn't crack a smile. "Do I look like I'm joking? Chop-chop." She clapped a couple of times and turned away.

"A'ight," Jamie said. "Damn." He gulped down the champagne, then handed the empty red cup to me. "Hold on to this, Charlie." He ran back into the house.

"Charlie?" Zelda said.

I did my best impression of Charlie Chaplin, miming a cane and a shaky little walk.

"Aha. I assume he calls you that because you don't speak. What a perfect little monster. Now, why don't you tell me about this outfit of yours. You're an elderly animal of some sort."

"He's a silver fox," Alana said, appearing at Zelda's side along with Tyler.

Zelda pursed her lips. "I'm not sure I understand the reference."

"It's sorta like the male version of a cougar."

"Cougars? Like the cat?"

Alana and Tyler shared a look. I don't think any of us knew if Zelda was only pretending not to understand, as part of her Halloween persona, or if she really didn't understand. "A cougar's an older woman who gets it on with young men," Alana said. "Basically, what we all aspire to. A silver fox is an older man who knows how to work the young ladies. And I'm Alana, by the way."

"Zelda Fitzgerald, née Sayre." Zelda gave a little curtsy. "Charmed to make your acquaintance."

"Uh, same."

Zelda took hold of my wig and gave it a little tug. "Well, I like the silver anyway. Makes you look distinguished."

Jamie came back from the kitchen with an armful of glasses.

"Those are for wine, not champagne!" Zelda shook her head. "But I suppose they'll have to do." She raised her glass to be filled, then made the toast. "To youth," she said.

"To youth," we all repeated.

I'd never had champagne before. It was a lot fizzier than I'd expected. I held some in my mouth and it seemed to evaporate, leaving a cloud of sweet air behind.

DRINK #4:
ANOTHER GLASS
OF BUBBLY

WHILE GLASSES WERE BEING REFILLED, I went to get the sunflowers, which I'd left on the lawn next to the keg. Two of the blossoms had been trampled into yellow mush, but the others were intact.

"For me?" Zelda asked. She laughed, then took the flowers out of my hand and put her nose into one of their big brown centers. "Well, I can honestly say I've never been given a bouquet of sunflowers. And you have no idea how rare it is for someone to surprise me." She kissed me on the cheek again, though this time I felt the corner of her mouth graze the corner of mine. "Now let's dance."

Sunflowers held aloft like a torch, Zelda led us all back into the house. The living room was packed with dancers, moving in sync like one gigantic, many-limbed organism. I've always liked dancing—probably because communication between bodies is always speechless, so my disability more or less disappears. Zelda was a strange dancer, moving in a way that once again brought to mind that comment I'd gotten on my old history paper: *anachronistic*. She didn't seem bothered by the fact that nobody else in the room was dancing the way she was, and though she got a few sidelong glances, they were the good kind of sidelong glance, the kind that said, *Man, that girl over there is dancing pretty weird, but I can tell she's not doing it because she has to be the center of attention by acting different, but because that is just the crazy-ass way she dances, because she is her own unique, magical, beautiful self, and she doesn't give a fuck what anybody else thinks, and any boy in here would be lucky as hell to be her dance partner tonight.*

I should add that I was definitely starting to feel drunk.

The crowd kept pushing Zelda and me closer and closer together, until our bodies met and there was nowhere to put my arms but around her. She was sparkly with sweat, swinging like a crystal chandelier in a hurricane. When the DJ finally put on a slow song, Zelda molded herself to me, so that I could feel each breath she took as a warm pressure against my chest. I looked over to Alana, who had Tyler's big hands placed perfectly on her butt cheeks. We made eye contact, and she gave me a subtle thumbs-up, mouthing the words, *Well done, Santé.*

DRINK #5:
A SWIG FROM A BOTTLE OF $1,000 SCOTCH

WE EXHAUSTED OURSELVES OVER THE course of the next hour, mashing our bodies into a liquid. Between her unique moves on the dance floor and all that champagne, Zelda already had Alana and company in the palm of her hand. I could tell they were seeing me in a new light now; I felt like a pitted little moon that had just been discovered orbiting a supernova.

"I'm tired of being cooped up," Zelda declared in the brief silence between songs. "How about we take this party down to the water?"

Another cheer went up. If she'd suggested we move the festivities to Brazil, everyone probably would've gone along with it. The limousine was still parked outside, so ten of us smushed inside while the rest of the partygoers trekked over to the N Judah, the train line that connects the San Francisco Bay to the Pacific Ocean. I ended up having to sit apart from Zelda, who was talking up a storm with Jamie and his friends.

I felt my phone vibrate in my pocket.

Who is this girl?! Alana had texted me.

I looked up and saw her sitting across the limo from me. She raised an eyebrow.

She's Zelda, I wrote back.

That's her costume, but who is she really?

Her name's really Zelda.

But she told me she's dressed up as Zelda Fitzgerald for Halloween.

Who?

F. Scott Fitzgerald's wife. We studied her in American history, remember? The Jazz Age?

I think I slept through that one.

It hadn't even occurred to me that "Zelda" might be some kind of pseudonym, but it wasn't as if I'd seen her driver's license or anything. And now that I thought about it, it *did* make for a pretty weird coincidence, and one having nothing to do with some rando historical figure: here was this girl very much in need of rescue—given her insistence that she was going to jump off a bridge any minute now—who just *happened* to have the same name as a famous video-game princess perpetually in need of saving. What were the odds?

Then again, Zelda hadn't actually asked for my help. In fact, *she* was the one helping *me*—buying me clothes and making me look cool and trying to get me to apply to college. It reminded me of this conversation we'd had in my eleventh-grade Life Skills class. Our teacher, Ms. Northrup, spent a whole period lecturing about "damaging stereotypes in popular culture" like "the damsel in distress." She asked us what kind of boring life Super Mario would have led if he hadn't had someone to rescue all the time:

"Princess Peach saved him every bit as much as he saved her," she'd said. "The guy was a plumber, for God's sake. He'd have been clearing out stopped-up toilets all day if not for Peach."

So probably Zelda hadn't named herself after Princess Zelda as some kind of cry for help (besides, she didn't seem like the type of girl with an in-depth knowledge of video games). But I still had no idea where the costume ended and the real person began. What if this new Southern accent *wasn't* fake, and it was the *other* accent—the bland, American non-accent I'd known up until now—that was put on?

"My darlings," Zelda suddenly announced, "please raise your hand if you are under twenty-five years of age." All of us raised our hands, smashing them against the ceiling of the limousine. "That's what I thought." She leaned over and opened the wooden cabinet mounted in the partition separating us from the driver's compartment. Inside was a tall green box on which was written THE GLENLIVET XXV. Zelda unsealed the top of the box and removed a large bottle full of amber liquid. She cradled it like a baby. "The heavenly beverage we are about to consume costs approximately one thousand dollars a bottle. And do you know why?"

"Because it's mad old," Jamie said.

"Exactly right, my carbuncular friend." Jamie grinned at this recognition of his wisdom. "Many years before your mommies and your daddies got the bright idea to spend an evening conceiving you, this divine potation was already resting peaceably in an aged oaken cask. While you were taking your first awkward steps around the living room, this paragon of whiskies was absorbing the flavor of that aged oaken cask, becoming richer and more complex with every passing hour. And all that time, as you grew into toddlers and schoolchildren, as you passed beyond the thorny gates of puberty and came to stand here on the very threshold of adulthood, the whiskey in that cask was slowly but constantly evaporating. They call it the angels' share, the portion that disappears over the years." Zelda peeled away the black wax that covered the top of the bottle and removed the stopper. She took a deep whiff and sighed with contentment. "Like many things in life, alcohol famously gets better and better with age. Yet we mustn't forget that something is also lost as time passes. We all must surrender our angel's share."

The limo had gone silent. Zelda was the kind of girl who could demand attention no matter what she said, but I think we were all a little in awe of her eloquence at that moment. The car filled with the peaty barbecue smell of the whiskey. Zelda drank first, straight from the bottle. She closed her eyes. We waited, spellbound, for her verdict.

"Paradise," she said, then passed the bottle to me. "Drink up, darling."

None of us were connoisseurs, of course. We wouldn't have known a twenty-five-year scotch from a twelve-year scotch from a watered-down jug of Jack Daniel's. But we all did as she'd done, swishing the liquid around our mouths with our eyes closed. A couple of people coughed, as if they were smoking for the first time. We all felt like we'd been let in on a secret.

DRINK #6:
THE LAST SWALLOW OF THE BOTTLE OF $1,000 SCOTCH

THE LIMO DROPPED US OFF DOWN BY THE Java Beach Café, where the N Judah turned around and trundled back toward downtown. Everyone who hadn't been able to fit in the limo would be taking the trolley, so the ten of us had some time on our own. We passed through a narrow rift between two big mountains of sand topped with tall waving grass. The night sky was clear, and the ocean was a black mirror sprinkled with a million tiny whitecap minnows. Without discussing it, we began to build the requisite bonfire. Stones for the outer ring were taken from fires that had already burned out. Finding the necessary driftwood required ranging up and down the beach. To the north, you could see where Great Highway curved up and around Point Lobos, culminating in the palatial luminosity of Cliff House. Down below, rocky caves filled with foam, like a fresh bottle of champagne uncorked every few seconds. We weren't alone on the beach—there were a few couples walking hand in hand, and far away you could see some other fires already blazing—but the vibe was peaceful and desolate. Everyone seemed content to let the crash of waves be the loudest thing on the beach. I brought an armful of kindling back to the circle. Alana and Zelda were digging the pit out with their hands, laughing about something. Back toward the highway, Tyler and Jamie were struggling with a log nearly as big as themselves.

Tyler dropped his end just as I was coming up to help. "This shit's too big to carry."

Jamie dropped his end too. "That's what your mom said."

In spite of myself, I laughed. Jamie gave me a funny look. "What are you doing, Charlie? Are you laughing?"

"Don't be a dick, man," Tyler said.

"But it's freaky! Anyway, I'm glad he's here." He put a sandy hand on my shoulder. "Parker, get real with me. What's the deal with your girl? You've got to be paying her, right?"

I shook my head.

"But there's no way you're hitting that." It wasn't a question, but a statement of fact. Obviously, someone beautiful and cool couldn't possibly want to be with me. If I were a different kind of person, I would've lied just to shut him up. But Zelda *wasn't* my girlfriend. Not yet, anyway.

I shook my head again.

"I knew it," Jamie said. "So you wouldn't mind if I stepped up." Another statement. "Good man." He clapped me hard on the back and headed toward the bonfire-to-be.

It took another ten minutes to round up the rest of the wood. Tyler oversaw the architecture of the thing: a boulder of crumpled-up newspaper, soaked in the contents of a couple of plastic Bic lighters; a Jenga-like structure of medium-size logs, packed in between with kindling; and then a teepee of big logs surrounding the whole thing. Alana did the honors of setting it alight. By the time the rest of the party came sprinting across the sand, the flames were going fierce and wild, shooting off little firework bursts every time a log settled and radiating heavy waves of heat to war against the chill.

Zelda snuck up behind me and pressed something into my hand.

"Hurry," she whispered. "Finish it before someone else does."

It was the thousand-dollar bottle of Scotch. I smiled and drank off what was left. Then I took Jamie's PS Vita from my jacket pocket and tossed it on the fire.

DRINK #7:
A MOUTHFUL OF SEAWATER

BY THIS TIME, IT WAS PROBABLY A GOOD thing I wasn't able to speak, because I doubt I could've put together a coherent sentence. The world came to me in flashes, like a flip book badly flipped. There was the sunburn heat of the fire on my face, the sand soft when I took my shoes and socks off, smoke in my lungs. I watched Jamie start a conversation with Zelda. He could be an asshole, but he was charming, too, the way a lot of assholes are. I felt drunkenly jealous—not because I thought anything would happen between them, but because now Jamie knew Zelda just as well as I did.

I wandered toward the water, down to where the sand turned wet enough to crunch between your toes. Even in the wan starlight, I could make out the circles that blossomed beneath every footfall. An exuberant wave crashed and sprinted up to burble over my skin. It burned at first, then prickled as hot blood filled the chilled veins.

"What a slimeball," Zelda said, bringing her pale little feet up close to mine. "He asked me if you were my community service project. I told him we'd been lovers for months. That you'd made me feel things I'd never felt before. That shut him up."

She smiled the kind of smile that wants a smile back, but I couldn't quite summon it up.

"Are you all right?"

I got down on my knees, dug my finger into the wet sand.

Who are you?

"You know who I am. I'm Zelda Fitzgerald. I'm a writer and a painter and a dancer. An all-around bon vivant straight out of the Jazz Age."

Seriously.

She sighed. "You wouldn't believe me if I told you."

Try me.

"Okay." Zelda hiked up her dress and knelt down next to me on the sand. When she wrote, she used two fingers, one a ghostly echo of the other, and drew in a long, looping cursive.

Name: Griselda Toth
DOB: 12/19/1770
Place of Birth: Kassel, G

We stood up just in time to watch the ocean rush over her words, filling in the curves like a dozen little moats, leaving only a few isolated letters behind.

I signed two letters at her: *B* and *S*.

"I told you you wouldn't believe me."

I can't explain how shitty it made me feel, that she still refused to tell me anything real about herself. My first date ever, and it was with a fictional character, or else a crazy person.

"Don't be blue, darling."

She reached out for me, but I stepped away.

"Oh, he's a moody boy," Zelda said. "But I know how to cheer him up." In one smooth motion, she pulled her black dress up over her head, taking the glittering headpiece with it. Like that, she was naked, white as the white feathers of a seagull, her hair almost blue in the moonlight. I was very suddenly very sober, and about 90 percent less angry.

"Well?" she said. "Your turn."

I'd never taken my clothes off in front of a girl before, but I was about four drinks past hesitation. The wig went first, coming to rest on the beach like some dried-up silver sea anemone. My shirt and jacket, then my pants. I waited for a moment, in my boxers that happened to have Pac-Man on them, to see if Zelda would turn around. She didn't. And now I could hear the whoops and hollers of the other partygoers, clued into what was going on and eager to join in. If I waited any longer, I'd end up putting on a show for all of them.

Boxers down.

Zelda took off toward the ocean, skipping like a long-legged crab, and I followed her. It was only a few steps before we were splashing in the shallows. The water was stupid cold and left us both gasping like freshly caught fish. We laughed hysterically at the sheer agony of it. Black rivers of mascara ran down Zelda's face. Back on the beach, everyone was tearing off their costumes piece by piece. It was like some kind of crazy dream, the sight of all those people emerging from their disguises, shedding the fake muscles and the plastic armor, the fairy wings and angel wings and devil horns, all of it piled up like a mass grave for make-believe, and I wondered if maybe this was a way for Zelda to show me something true, a version of herself without any clothes or makeup to hide behind. She slipped around me and clamped onto my back, holding her soft shivery self to my spine, wrapping her legs around my hips. She threw a lock of silver seaweed hair over my shoulder and whispered in my ear, "This has been a perfect night." Other people were splashing into the water now, screaming with the cold and the insanity of it. I turned to smile at Zelda and she kissed me, right on the mouth this time, and I kissed her back. I forgot to keep kicking and we sank like a stone.

I swallowed a mouthful of seawater.

DRINK #8:
A TAP-WATER CHASER

NOBODY COULD SURVIVE IN THAT WATER
for long. One by one, we lugged our frozen bodies back to shore,
dried ourselves off with our own dry clothes, and sat in a circle
around the bonfire. It was the quiet time that I've learned comes
at the end of every party, when tomorrow starts to rear its ugly
head in the imagination. The wood crackled. People smoked
and stared into the dying flames. When there was nothing left
but embers, Zelda and I tramped back to the parking lot, where
the limo was still waiting. We kissed again, and we didn't stop
until the car pulled up in front of my house.

"Home sweet home," Zelda said. "This is where we say
adieu."

I pointed at her, then at the house.

"You want me to come in? How modern! But won't your
parents mind?"

I shook my head, then mimed drinking followed by sleep.
Zelda still seemed uncertain, so I took her hand and pulled her
out of the car with me.

"Fine, fine, fine," she said. "I'll come of my own free will,
thank you."

She paid the limo driver (and how many of those hundreds had she spent to keep the guy there all night?), and then we went inside, padding as quietly as possible through the narrow kitchen and up the stairs. The ladder to the attic groaned as I lowered it, but I knew my mom wouldn't wake up.

It was weird, having a girl I liked in my room. Suddenly everything embarrassed me: Irrelephant the stuffed elephant, who sat on top of my bed against the pillows; the PlayStation 4 under the television; the science-fiction and fantasy novels prominently displayed on the bookshelf. Luckily, it was dark, and Zelda was drunk. We both changed out of our costumes. I gave her a T-shirt and boxers to wear, and she almost fell over trying to get them on. We slipped under the covers together.

"Parker?" I waited for her to remember that I couldn't answer her in words. "I'm not going to have sex with you tonight. You're very sweet and all, with your giant bouquet of sunflowers, and I really do like you, but it wouldn't be right. Even if it would be fun. And I'm very fun, by the way. *Very* fun." I watched as she struggled to catch back up with her train of thought. "But that isn't relevant. I still can't sleep with you. It's not about the sex, you see, but about everything that comes with it. Do you understand?" Though Zelda had asked me the question, I got the feeling she was actually arguing with herself. Her voice was getting more and more frantic. "I can't just start all over again, Parker. I'm burned out. I'm a shell! It wouldn't be remotely fair to you, or to him, or even to me." She took hold of my head with both of her hands, stared hard into my eyes. "Not fair at all, Parker Santé."

I had no idea what she was talking about, or who she'd been referring to when she said "him." Did that mean she had a boyfriend?

Suddenly she let go of my cheeks and fell onto her back, laughing. "I keep expecting you to answer. But you can't, can you?" She sat up on an elbow. "You know, some people would say you're every woman's fantasy. A man who can only listen." It was the first time anyone other than my mom had ever referred to me as a man (and when my mom said it, it was always "young man," with the ironic implication that I wasn't doing justice to the title). Weirdly, just the word kinda made me feel like one.

"I'm sure it'll all make sense in the morning," she said, calm now. She rested her head against my chest, and a few seconds later, she was asleep. I let her lie there for a while, trying my best not to move. But pretty soon my arm turned numb and prickly, and there was still a bad taste in the back of my throat from all that alcohol. Zelda snorted a little when I rolled her off me.

I was downstairs drinking a big glass of tap water when I heard it. Distant music, like one of those ice cream trucks that are always chugging around the city during the summer. I thought it was coming from outside, but as I walked back up the stairs, the sound only got louder. It wasn't until I was back in the attic that I understood what I was hearing.

Zelda's phone was ringing.

I opened up her purse and pulled it out. The ringing finally stopped. I looked over at Zelda, to see if she'd heard anything, but she was dead to the world. A second later the phone dinged. Voice mail.

I pressed the button before I had time to think about it.

"Ms. Toth, this is Gabby Greene at the UCSF Medical Center. I'm calling about Nathaniel. Please contact us as soon as you can. It's urgent."

Fucked up, I know, to listen to someone's voice mail. But you know what's even more fucked up? Deleting that voice mail, then going into the missed call log and deleting the record that the call ever came in, then going into the phone's settings and putting the phone on "Do Not Disturb" mode, so no other calls would come in.

And sure, it was likely that she'd been bullshitting me all along (though the voice mail did bear out two things she'd told me—that her last name was Toth, and that she had some sort of connection to a man named Nathaniel), and that whatever the message was about, it would not result in her jumping off the Golden Gate Bridge. But there was also a tiny sliver of a chance that by doing what I'd just done, I'd saved her life. And maybe my own, too.

I crawled back into bed and passed out.

SATURDAY, NOVEMBER

1

WHAT'S IN THE BOX?

I WOKE UP WITH A HEAD FULL OF COTTON balls spiked with broken glass. Every thud of my heartbeat felt like a monkey smacking my brain with a Ping-Pong paddle. Then I remembered the girl in my bed, and the monkey calmed down a bit. Her eyes opened: Pacific Ocean in one, Atlantic in the other. I was afraid she would freak out when she realized she'd spent the night with me.

"Good morning." She smiled sleepily, then winced. "Oh my. I can't remember the last time I had a hangover. We must have coffee, and quickly."

We groaned our way out of bed. Zelda didn't have any other clothes with her, so she ended up in my T-shirt and hoodie, along with the skinny black jeans she'd bought for me at the mall (which fit her surprisingly well). She was getting one of her socks out from under the bed when she found the box.

"What's this?"

I'd almost forgotten it was there. A couple of years ago, my dad's publisher had sent back a whole bunch of his unpublished work. I guess they'd been thinking about doing some kind of omnibus or something (final verdict: no thanks). My mom said she couldn't bear to read any of it, so she'd just given it all to me.

D-a-d, I finger spelled.

Zelda looked confused. "Bab?"

D-a-d, I signed again, mouthing the word at the same time.

"Oh! Your dad! This is his work?"

I nodded.

She knelt down next to the box and pulled off the lid, revealing a chaos of papers and file folders and notebooks. Some pages were written in a dense, incomprehensible cursive. Others had been typed on a typewriter. There were pieces in Spanish and pieces in English. There were newspaper clippings and old photographs and a few bound journals labeled *Diario*.

"His diaries," Zelda said, holding one up. "Have you read these?"

I shook my head. I'd tried once, back when the box first arrived, but the time it took to decipher the scrawl of his handwriting wasn't worth the boring adult problems he'd written about. Zelda flipped through one of the journals and stopped at a random page.

"June fifteenth, 2005," she read. "It's the same old fight. She says there needs to be more money, I say there will be soon. She says she doesn't mind working, I say I do mind." I had no idea Zelda knew Spanish; to be translating on the fly like this was impressive. "And then one of us is shouting, then the other is shouting, then I break something that I can't afford to break.

Then I go for a walk to clear my head, only my head doesn't clear." She stopped reading, then set the diary back in the box and replaced the lid. "I'm sorry. I shouldn't have done that."

I grabbed my journal and a pen from my desk.

It's nothing I don't already know, I wrote. *He was pretty unhappy.*

"So I see. Why do you think that was?"

I guess he wasn't as successful as he wanted to be. His last book sold about two hundred copies.

"Wasn't he good?"

I don't know. But maybe he didn't work as hard as he could have. I remember my mom and I came home this one day, and I closed the front door too loudly, and he came running out of his office. This was in the house we used to have, which was way bigger. And he got all angry about how he needed quiet to work. But a while later, I looked through the keyhole, and he was just sitting there playing solitaire and drinking a beer.

"Maybe that was part of his process."

I gave Zelda a *yeah right* look, so I didn't have to write it.

"Did he ever hurt you?"

Not like that. He wasn't a bad guy. I think I'm making it sound like he was.

"There are no bad guys," Zelda said, putting her hand on mine. "Only in bad movies."

I slid the box back under the bed. We finished getting dressed and climbed down from the attic. I could hear my mom banging around in the kitchen below us. We'd have to find some way around her.

"This is your mom and dad?" Zelda asked, gesturing to the half-dozen framed photos mounted along the wall. I nodded.

"My God, it's like a graveyard in here. Is that her bedroom?" Before I could say anything, Zelda had pushed open the door. My mom's bed was unmade, the pillow still cratered. Her drugs were on the bedside table—Prozac and Tylenol PM—alongside an empty bottle of wine. Zelda seemed more interested in all the photographs. One over the television. Another on the wall next to the windows. A couple propped up on her vanity. Zelda picked up the one right behind the Prozac. Inside a little flowered frame, my dad was sitting at a picnic table, smoking a cigarette. "How long ago did he die?"

I held up five fingers.

"And your mom never remarried?" I shook my head. "I shouldn't be surprised, I suppose. What man would want to make love in a house full of ghosts?"

It felt deeply weird discussing my mom's personal life with a near stranger. Actually, it felt weird discussing my mom's personal life at all. I took Zelda's hand and pulled her back out into the hallway.

Stay here, I mouthed, once we reached the top of the stairs.

"Yes, sir," Zelda said with mock seriousness.

In the kitchen, my mom was standing at the stove. The

impossibly delicious smell of bacon went to work on my nostrils, momentarily distracting me from my task of getting Zelda out of the house unseen.

"Morning, sunshine," my mom said. I tried to sidle past her into the living room. "Hold on a second." She put one hand on the back of my head and used the other to pull my eyelid down, staring at the crackly redness under my pupil. "You're hungover!" she announced.

Like I said, it's really hard to lie when you can't speak. I was composing my explanation when both of us were distracted by the telltale creak of something on the stairs. I looked at my mom. She looked at the stairs. I looked at the stairs. My mom looked at me. I looked at her. We both looked at the stairs.

"Good morning, Ms. Santé," Zelda said. "I'm Zelda."

There is a kind of shock that paralyzes your usual response systems, like when someone says something so totally dickish to you that you can't think of a coherent comeback until hours later. I could see that my mom was experiencing exactly that kind of shock. Most kids would get in serious trouble for getting drunk and bringing home some random girl; but for me, it represented such a giant leap toward normal teenage behavior, I knew that my mom wouldn't be able to condemn it. She was stuck between two impossible reactions. The moment stretched out, on and on, underscored by the sizzle of bacon.

"I guess I'll have to scramble more eggs," my mom said.

"Thank you, Ms. Santé."

Zelda and I went into the living room and sat down. I left a whole couch cushion between us—a pretty empty gesture toward modesty, given what my mom must have assumed had already happened last night (but which, tragically, had not). Breakfast was served a few minutes later, along with life-giving coffee.

"We need anything else?" my mom asked.

"This all looks wonderful," Zelda said.

"Oh, good."

There would be no avoiding it now. It was inevitable, like death and taxes and *Law & Order* being on television at any given point in the day. My mom sat down in the easy chair across from us, took a deep breath, and then . . .

THE INTERROGATION, PART 1

"SO, ZELDA, TELL ME ALL ABOUT YOURSELF. Where are you from?"

"Omaha," Zelda said, without hesitation. And was it just me, or had she just taken on a shade of a Nebraskan accent? "Have you ever been?"

"I have, actually. I'm a flight attendant for Delta Airlines, so I've been all over."

"That must be fun. I've always found flying so romantic."

My mom laughed. "Romantic? Maybe fifty years ago, back when air travel was just for rich people. But those days are long gone."

"What a shame. You know, American Airlines used to have a piano bar in *coach*. Can you imagine? Now you're lucky if you get a bag of peanuts. And even when you do, it's impossible to open."

"Sounds like you've traveled a lot. You an army brat or something?"

Zelda shook her head. "I suppose I have an incurable case of wanderlust. It's like Kundera said: 'In the mind of a woman for whom no place is home the thought of an end to all flight is unbearable.'"

My mom looked bewildered, and I could sympathize—talking to Zelda could be a trippy experience. "So where do you go to school?"

"The Lycée Français, downtown. Do you know it?"

Last night, Zelda had told me that she didn't go to school at all. So had she been lying then, or was she lying now?

"Of course! How fancy!" My mom put on a terrible French accent. *"Parlez-vous?"*

"Bien sûr! Et vous?"

"Oh, uh, no. Not really. A bit of Spanish is all."

"Me gusta español tambien."

My mom reached over and smacked me on the kneecap. "What an accomplished young woman you've got here, Parky!"

Don't I know it, I signed.

"And where are you planning to go to college, Zelda?"

"Mostly the same places that Parker is applying, actually."

Shit! My mom was never supposed to know about the bargain Zelda and I had struck, mostly because I had no intention of carrying out my side of it. I stared laser-beam death eyes at Zelda, but she went blithely on. "Yeah, things are going so well between us, I figure why not try to stay together at university."

My mom had this look on her face like she'd just won the lottery. "This is news to me! Last I heard, he wasn't applying at all."

"He didn't want you to make some big deal about it," Zelda

said. "With his grades and all, he might not be accepted. But I thought you should know."

"Well—this—I—"

At first I thought my mom was just at a loss for words, then I realized she had started to cry. "I'm sorry, Parker," she blubbered, "but this is such huge news. And I just wish . . . I just wish Marco was here. He'd—"

"No doom and gloom this morning, Ms. Santé," Zelda said, managing to interrupt the sobfest before it could really get going. "We should be celebrating! Do you have any music in here?" She scanned the room until she found the stereo on the shelf below the television. "Perfect."

She switched it on and turned the station to some fast, old-timey jazz.

"Come on," she said, putting out a hand to me. "I spent all last night dancing to the music you like. Now it's your turn."

I stood up, and she immediately pulled me close. We danced cheek to cheek, with one arm held straight out as if we were pulling back the string of a bow together.

"I love this kind of music!" my mom said. She wiped at her eyes, then stood up and began bopping around the room in an adorable old-person sort of way. After thirty seconds or so, she collapsed back onto the couch. "I'm too old for dancing."

"Nonsense!" Zelda said. "You're not even the oldest person in the room!"

My mom laughed, mostly out of confusion, and before long

started to dance again. The three of us kept on going like that for a good twenty minutes, and I realized this was maybe the purest, most uncomplicated joy there'd been inside the house for a long time.

IN THE JAPANESE TEA GARDEN

I KNOW THIS MIGHT BE HARD TO BELIEVE, but back in elementary school, before I became the famously speechless recluse I am today, I actually had a best friend. His name was John, and we spent every available minute playing together in Golden Gate Park. We would pretend to be wizards and warriors from our favorite video games, wielding dead branches as swords and lobbing pinecones as if they were fireballs. It didn't take us long to colonize every area of the park, like some upstart imperial power planting its flag in an already inhabited land. I still have some of the maps we drew up, with all their tantalizing geographic inventions: Goblin's Graveyard, the Terrortory, the Lake of Giant Piranha, Singed Mountain. Across these landscapes we waged an epic and unending war against a nameless evil, which is to say we ran around kicking and punching at the air for a few minutes at a time and then declaring victory. To everyone else in the park, it probably looked as if two kids were simultaneously having a twenty-minute epileptic seizure. But in our heads, we were nothing short of heroes.

John and I stopped hanging out once we got to middle school, but I kept playing make-believe on my own up to an age I'm not, at this moment, willing to put down in writing. So Zelda couldn't believe it when I told her I'd never been inside the Japanese Tea Garden, which was located smack in the middle of Golden Gate Park, just behind a set of big red lacquered doors. The six-dollar entrance fee had always been enough to put me off, as the rest of the park was open to the public for free. But Zelda said it was one of her favorite spots in the city, and after our impromptu dance party with my mom, we headed there together, past the post-Halloween walk-of-shame parade.

A teenage girl dressed all in black sat inside the tea garden ticket booth, reading a magazine that appeared to consist entirely of photographs of tattoos.

"Two, please," Zelda said.

Beyond the gates, bridges arched steeply over clear ponds. Tiny, perfectly trimmed trees twisted their trunks as if wringing out a wet towel. The bright-red skeletons of Japanese maples shed their leaves like confetti—pink on one side and white on the other. The teahouse was at the center of the garden. Only a half-dozen people or so were spread out over the wooden patio, talking quietly and sipping at steaming ceramic cups. We took a seat at a table overlooking a rocky creek. When the waitress came by, Zelda ordered for both of us.

I pulled out my journal and started to write. I had more questions than ever after Zelda's Oscar-worthy performance at breakfast.

So was what you told my mom about Omaha and the French school true? I wrote.

"No. I told you the truth last night. Or I tried to, anyway."

I'm serious.

Zelda sighed. "Parker, let's play a game, okay? It's called Benefit of the Doubt. It's the game that all people play when they meet someone new. If a girl tells you she's from Australia, or she's an acrobat, you just believe her, don't you? You don't assume she's lying."

Saying you're from Australia isn't the same as saying you're two hundred years old.

"Two hundred and forty-six, Parker, and sure it is, if it's the truth."

So prove it.

"That's easier said than done, believe me. What could I show you that would convince you?"

I thought about that and realized she was right. It wasn't like I could chop her down and count the rings.

"How about this—would you agree that I'd have to be a pretty impressive person to make up a convincing story of immortality?"

You _are_ a pretty impressive person, I wrote.

Zelda smiled. "Ask me anything. Try and catch me in a lie. I dare you."

The tea arrived. Genmaicha, it was called. I've always liked the smell of tea a lot more than the taste, so I spent a second just breathing in the pungent smoke that rose from the cup. When I finally sipped, I was surprised; it tasted like burnt rice. Not bad.

I can really ask you anything?

"Do your worst."

I always do.

WHERE WERE YOU BORN? I WROTE.

"A small city in Germany called Kassel. Very beautiful at the time, though you'd never know it now. The city center was destroyed during the war."

The war?

"World War II. One hundred and fifty thousand people displaced in a single night."

I reached for my phone and looked up Kassel on Wikipedia. Zelda waited patiently while I read. Everything checked out, so I searched the page for something more obscure to ask her.

Tell me about the Bergpark Wilhelmshöhe, I wrote, glad I didn't have to worry about my pronunciation.

"It's an enormous park built on a hillside. Every year, they would run water out of the Hercules monument and down to the lake around the castle. We children would chase it all the way there."

And can you tell me some famous people who've lived in Kassel?

"The Brothers Grimm are probably the best known. They did all their best work in the city, though I wasn't living there at the time. I did meet them at a party once. One was frightfully dull, and the other was frightfully gay. Of course, such things weren't discussed in those days. Homosexuality, that is. Not being dull."

Which painter is featured in the palace there?

"There are a few, but you probably mean Rembrandt. Not my favorite. Too dark."

Okay, so maybe this line of questioning wasn't panning out, but it's not like it would have been hard for her to memorize the Wikipedia page for one little town.

She smiled with a hint of triumph. "So are you convinced yet?"

You're just answering trivia questions.

"Only because you're asking trivia questions."

She was right. Hard facts were easy. I needed something bigger, something harder to fabricate.

Tell me your life, I wrote.

"My life?"

Yeah. Like, the whole thing all at once.

"Two hundred and fifty years makes for a pretty long story."

You said two hundred and forty-six.

"I was rounding!" Zelda sighed. "Voltaire said that the secret of being a bore is to tell everything. You don't know this yet, Parker, but it's possible to get sick of your own stories. Is this the only thing that will satisfy you?"

Stop stalling and talk.

"My, my! What a little dictator!" Zelda picked up her tea

and blew on it, then took a slow sip. I figured that would be time enough for a good storyteller to come up with the basic outline of a fiction, but there would still be holes, if I listened closely enough. There were always holes in a first draft.

"My father was a judge," she finally said. "My mother was a mother, as all mothers were back then. My childhood was relatively normal for the time. I was educated in the things that girls such as myself were allowed to be educated in. Music and drawing. Languages. The niceties. I was a catch, even with this." She pointed at her silver hair. "Yes, it's always looked like that."

You dyed it.

"Oh you're such a *man*. Look at the roots, silly. The color goes all the way down."

She leaned over the table and stuck her head in my face. I reached forward and separated a couple of strands. It was true—silver from top to bottom.

You could've had it done yesterday, I wrote.

"Yes," Zelda scoffed. "I dyed my hair yesterday so I could convince you, a boy I'd yet to meet, that my hair was naturally silver. Don't be ridiculous." She flipped her hair back over her head. "Anyway, my first husband, Karl, quite liked the color. He said it was a mark of distinction. We were married when I was eighteen. Karl was a lawyer, a very good friend of my father's. I liked him well enough, and I did my best to be a good wife. But it turns out that one of the symptoms of my condition is an inability to conceive. We tried everything. I spent months at a time in sanatoriums at very high altitudes. 'Taking the waters,' as it was called. When it became clear that there would be no cure, my husband had our marriage annulled. I figured I would never marry again. In those days a woman who couldn't bear children was hardly a woman at all. I stayed at home with my mother and father while my siblings all started families of their own. It was another few years before the questions began. Why did I look the same at twenty-five as I had at eighteen? Why did I look the same at twenty-eight? At thirty-three? People still believed in witches and demons back then, you see. When the gossip grew too loud to ignore, my father moved me to a house we kept in Scotland. There was no one there but a housekeeper and a groundskeeper. Fiona and Clive, they were called. Eventually they came to understand my condition, but discretion was still considered a virtue in those days, and neither of them ever said a word. Such beautiful souls, they were. I saw both of them put in the ground."

Zelda stared off into space, teacup poised against her bottom lip, steam floating in front of her eyes like mist on a lake. She appeared to be on the brink of tears. I still didn't believe her, of course, but I was increasingly impressed by both her stubborn dedication to the story and her dramatic ability.

"Life in Scotland was dreary, but at least I was safe. If I had to go into town, I'd cover my face with a scarf, but mostly I stayed in. I read books and tended my garden. I played music and painted. Decades passed. My siblings came to visit me a few times over the years, and one of my sisters even lived with me for a while, but eventually they all passed away. Not long after I turned one hundred, I began to travel. I visited dozens of countries all across the world, on every continent but Antarctica. Around the turn of the twentieth century, I decided to move to America. It was much easier to falsify documents back then, so I was able to reinvent myself as my own descendant. I couldn't do that now, of course. Technology has sucked the magic out of so many things."

How do you survive? I wrote.

"My family left me money, which ran out around the time of the Great Depression. I took jobs after that, until I got married again, to Nathaniel. I mentioned him to you yesterday, I think. We met at the Palace Hotel. He was a handsome young man, but I'd known a lot of handsome young men in my time, so I was cautious. It took months of persuasion on his part before I agreed to have dinner with him. We were married within the year, and soon after, we left America and began to travel the world together."

The name Nathaniel reminded me of the voice mail I'd deleted last night. He was definitely a real person, but God only knew why Zelda was pretending he was her husband.

Did you tell him all the same stuff you're telling me?

"Of course. He was bound to catch on sooner or later."

And he believed you?

"He did." Zelda drank off the rest of her tea. "Now, do you have any more questions, Parker Santé, or are you ready to admit defeat?"

I considered. She'd done as good a job as anyone could have; I hadn't spotted a single hole in her story. But that hardly mattered when the story she was trying to sell me involved immortality, multiple marriages, and hanging out with the Brothers Grimm. Basically, the whole thing was a hole.

Sorry, I wrote. *But no.*

BELIEVE IT

"WELL, I DON'T KNOW WHAT ELSE TO TELL
you," Zelda said. "I've done everything I can."

I write stories too, Zelda. It's not that hard.

"It is for me. I don't have that talent. I can only tell things
as they are."

*But you don't actually expect me to believe you're immortal just
because you say so, do you? I'm not stupid.*

"I don't think you're stupid, Parker, and I didn't say I was
immortal. I just don't seem to age. I have every confidence that
when I jump off the Golden Gate Bridge, that will be the end
of things."

*See, there you go again. More crazy shit you want me to believe
just because I like you. You say you're going to kill yourself so I'll
feel sorry for you or something, and you make up this husband—*

Zelda reached across the table and ripped out the page of
the journal I'd been writing on. She crumpled it up into a ball
and tossed it over the railing, into the stream. She was angry
now, or pretending to be anyway; I could almost see the waves
crashing in her eyes.

"Parker, do you want me to leave?"

Her tone was dead serious, and I suddenly remembered this vacation my mom and dad had taken me on, back when I was really little. We'd spent a whole week fishing off some huge boat in Alaska, along with a bunch of other people and this really intense fisherman-captain dude whose beard was so thick you probably could've hidden a full-grown salmon in it. The trip was crazy boring up until the third day, when I got my first bite. All at once, everybody on deck started cheering, and this fish was thrashing around for its smelly life, and I was pulling and pulling, and the line was jumping like an EKG during a heart attack, and the intense fisherman-captain dude was watching with this look on his face like he would be evaluating my viability as a human being based on whether or not I landed this stupid fish. I fought and I fought and I fought . . . and then everything went slack. The cheering died. The fisherman turned away. I'd lost the fish.

And you'd think I wouldn't have given a shit. I mean, so I didn't have a fish, right? Who cared? One minute earlier, I hadn't had a fish either. But somehow that one minute of struggle had transformed the very concept of not having a fish, from something that didn't matter at all to something that mattered a whole lot.

If I'd never met Zelda, well, that would have been one thing. But now that I had her, or almost had her, I couldn't stand the idea of losing her. Which I realize makes it sound like

I'm comparing her to a fish. But whatever—it's a metaphor. Deal with it.

"Parker, do you want me to leave?" she asked.

I shook my head.

"Then you have to believe me. Because I'm not going to spend what is probably my last day on earth trying to convince someone I'm not a liar. I promise you that, in exchange, I'll believe everything you tell me as well, even though you're an admitted thief, misanthrope, school skipper, and all-around malcontent."

I'll try, I wrote on a fresh page.

"No. Not good enough." She pushed our cups of tea to the edge of the table. "Close your eyes."

Why?

"Just do it."

I did. And then I felt Zelda's hands come to rest gently on top of mine. "Believe, Parker."

So I thought back over everything I now "knew" about Zelda. She didn't age. She'd been born in 1770 in Germany. She'd been married twice—and unless there were *two* Nathaniels in her life, one of those husbands was in the hospital just down the street.

No one had ever been fed a more unbelievable story.

Believe it, I told myself. *Believe it.*

I opened my eyes.

"So?" she said. "Do you?"

I nodded, and even if I only about 25 percent meant it, Zelda was so happy she leaned across the table and kissed me. It was probably only a 3 on the passion scale (with our full-on skinny-dip make-out the previous night a 9.5), but it was the first time we'd kissed that day, and thus a powerful motivator toward blind faith in the impossible—say 33 percent now.

"Glad we got that sorted out," she said, then opened up her purse and dropped another hundred-dollar bill on the table. The wad was a little bit thinner than it had been yesterday, and I had this image of Zelda as a tree, losing her leaves one by one, until nothing but naked branches were left. "Let's go for a walk, shall we? I think it's high time *you* told some stories."

WE AMBLED ALONG THE GRAVEL PATHS THAT crisscrossed the tea garden. Every crunch of our feet sounded like a big dog taking a bite out of something.

"I have so many things I want to ask you," Zelda said. "But your condition being what it is, we can't really walk and talk at once, can we?"

I shook my head. It was one of the many downsides of communicating through the written word, along with writer's cramp and the fact that you needed a paper shredder to keep your past conversations secret.

"That's all right. We'll just have to alternate. I'll ask you something, and then you can stop somewhere and write down your answer while I do a lap of the park. When I get back, I'll sit down and read your answer while you walk a lap. Sound good?"

I nodded.

"First question: What was your first kiss like? Be as detailed as possible."

She skipped off over one of those steep bridges, and I sat down on a stone bench. I've already told you about Rosie Cuevas and the game of spin the bottle, so I won't bother copying down exactly what I wrote (I've still got the journal, complete but for the page Zelda threw in the stream, so it's possible to recreate my half of our conversations word for word). It's not much of a story, so I was finished with it long before Zelda got back to the bench. I left her there to read, walking a random path through the park, passing cuddly young couples and their slow-moving elderly counterparts. I got a little lost on the way back, and Zelda greeted me by chucking the journal at my head. I barely caught it by the front cover.

"Well, that was boring," she said.

I put on an offended expression.

She sighed. "I suppose I should have asked a more exciting question. For example, why don't you tell me about the first person you ever slept with."

She started to walk away, so I had to jump up and grab her shoulder.

"What?"

I haven't, I wrote.

"Haven't what?"

I spread out my hands in the universal gesture for *Figure it out, genius.*

"Oh!" She laughed, which made me feel about four years old. "I'm sorry, Parker. I just thought all the kids were doing it these days. Another question, then. Have you ever been in love?"

I shook my head.

"My God. Who gets to seventeen without falling in *or* making love?"

I shrugged. What was there to say?

"Well, this romantic angle is proving entirely fruitless. Family, then. Can you tell me what happened to your father?"

That's kinda hard for me.

"Well, I've told you all *my* secrets. It's only fair you give me something of yours. Besides, if you're going to be a writer, you have to be able to talk about the deep stuff."

Fine. I'll try.

"Take your time. I'll walk slowly."

I decided not to overthink it. I'd just set down the facts as I remembered them. To let too much emotional stuff in would result in a Golden-Gate-Park-size bummer of a story, and I was trying to keep things with Zelda light.

We were driving back from the East Bay IKEA, I wrote. *We'd just merged from the 80 to the 101. I remember I was licking that IKEA-brand ice cream (Yogurt? Fro-yo? Vanilla-flavored chemical mush? What is that shit, anyway?) off the little web between my thumb and index finger. My dad had just wrapped up some argument with my mom on the phone. Maybe he forgot to buy something, or else he bought something he wasn't supposed to. I don't know. I was twelve and I had ice cream, so nothing else really mattered.*

My dad was angry, but I was used to that. He was angry a lot. And whenever he got angry, he ended up breaking something.

Just things, though. Never people. "It's only stuff," he would say, right after putting his foot through a door or smashing a plate against a wall. Maybe we were at IKEA that day replacing something he'd broken. That would make a lot of sense, actually.

Anyway, you must know what it's like driving with someone who's pissed off. They accelerate too quickly. They steer in these angry little jerks. They swear at every other car on the road—like the one that had just pulled up alongside us. Six teenagers were packed into this shitty red Jetta, and we were trying to get over into their lane so we could take the off-ramp, only this other car kept changing speed to match us, and the driver was laughing his head off because he knew exactly what he was doing (turns out he'd had just enough to put him over the limit). My dad put his foot to the floor, but we were in the old Tercel, which accelerated like a fucking turtle on NyQuil. I guess he thought he was clear, or that the asshole kid would back off. But when he changed lanes, we caught the other car's front bumper, and suddenly we were swerving to the right, and then there was this huge crash and everything started spinning.

I don't know if I blacked out or what, but when I was aware of being a person again, I felt this weird weight in my head, kinda like when you've got a bad cold. It took me a while to realize it was because I was hanging upside down from my seat belt. My door looked like crumpled-up tinfoil. I looked over at my dad and his eyes were fluttering, and there was blood running down his seat belt toward the roof of the car. The windows were all shattered, but I could see the shadows of cars rushing by, and I remember thinking how weird it was that the world wasn't just stopping in its tracks for us. We were flipped over in the middle of the highway and my dad was dripping onto the fucking roof, you know? But I think life is a little like one of those special memory-foam mattresses that they advertise on TV, where you can drop a bowling ball on one side and the person sleeping a few inches away doesn't feel a thing. Our biggest tragedies are still just ours. There's this short story by Ursula K. Le Guin called "The Ones Who Walk Away from Omelas." It's about this city where everyone is super happy and healthy and smart, but when the citizens reach a certain age, they're told that the perfect awesomeness of their city depends on one kid being kept in a dirty cellar, all alone, fed just enough crappy food not to starve. Everyone knows he's down there, but they also know that if they ever help him out, if they ever give him so much as a single chicken nugget, their whole society will collapse. It's one of those parable things, about all the unhappy people we ignore so that we can be happy. All the overturned cars we drive past without giving even a tiny bit of a shit about what's going on inside.

I wasn't sure if I was done or not, but when Zelda came back, I handed her the journal and pretty much ran away, because I didn't want to see her read it. And as I walked around the park again, I had this really strong urge to just leave her and the journal behind, because I knew that when I got back, things would be different between us. She would know me in a way that nobody but my mom and Dr. Milton really knew me. I stood at the entrance to the tea garden, staring out at the street, and about 49 percent of me was ready to bolt. Luckily, 51 percent of me wasn't a total idiot.

When I got back, Zelda was sitting on the bench with the journal closed on her lap, watching a couple canoodle on the grass down by the stream.

She looked up at me. "That was the deep stuff, Parker. Thank you."

I took the journal back. *Why is it that the bad shit in our lives always seems to take up so much more mental space than the good stuff?* I wrote. *Is that part of being a person, or just part of being me?*

"I think about that question all the time."

Do you have an answer?

"I don't think questions like that have answers. An optimistic person would probably say the bad things stick out because they're not as common as the good things."

Are you an optimistic person?

"No."

But you're not serious about the Golden Gate Bridge, are you?

"We had a deal, Parker. You were going to believe everything I said."

But why would you want to kill yourself? I mean, I hate pretty much everyone and everything, and I'm still not suicidal.

"I'm not suicidal. I'm just"—she struggled to find the words—"tired out."

With what?

"Life."

How can you be tired out with all of life?

"After a quarter of a millennia, the real question would be how could I *not* be tired out. It's just too much time, Parker. Why else do you think elderly people aren't constantly complaining about their imminent deaths? It's because they're ready, just like I am. Can't you understand that? Have you ever really thought about what it would be like to live forever?"

I hesitated, pen over the paper. Sure I'd thought about it, the same way I'd thought about being invisible or telepathic or able to fly. And I'd concluded that it would be awesome. All the things you could see and the people you could meet and the places you could go. All the time you'd have to learn how to play the guitar and to break dance, to act up and fuck up and hook up. All the days and months and years and decades, stretching out in front of you, like a highway running through an endless, desolate city . . .

You're right, I wrote. *It sounds kinda shitty.*

Zelda smiled. "Why?"

How to say it? Because life sucked a lot of the time. Because it already seemed long enough. Because I could remember visiting my dad's mom when she was dying of throat cancer in a hospital bed in a town outside of Bogotá, surrounded by dirty orange tiles and all those flickering fluorescent lights humming like bored orderlies, and how she kept saying *ya basta* whenever anyone asked how she was. Sometimes it was a joke, and sometimes it was so serious it made her cry. *Ya basta. No doy más.*

So we shared a popcorn yesterday, I wrote.

"That's true," Zelda said. "And your point is . . . ?"

The funny thing about popcorn is that you've really only got two options. There's the small, which has about six kernels of popcorn in it and costs $6.49 or something. And then you've got the medium and the large, which are both just ridiculously huge. A starving family couldn't eat that much popcorn in a week. But they only cost a few cents more than the small. I guess the theater is hoping you'll just think, like, fuck it, right? Fifty cents for a shit-ton more popcorn? Might as well. But the problem is that if you get the massive popcorn, you end up feeling gross, because it's too much. It doesn't leave you wanting more. And you can really only enjoy something if it leaves you wanting more, don't you think?

When Zelda finished reading my little essay, she let her head fall onto my shoulder. "I do, Parker. I really do."

We sat there in silence for a while, and I figured it didn't really matter if she was crazy, or depressed, or a compulsive liar, or all three at once. Something was wrong with her. Something was eating away at her from the inside. And I was going to save her from it. Like Mario saved Princess Peach. Like Link saved Zelda.

Okay, immortal girl, I wrote, *you say you're tired out with life, right? Well, I'm going to untire you. I'm going to make you want to live.*

"That's a tall order, Parker Santé."

I'm a tall guy.

She laughed, probably because I'm actually not very tall, and then I kissed her, the first time I'd initiated a kiss in my whole life. We kept on kissing for a long time, making everyone else in the Japanese Tea Garden jealous, or at the very least, super uncomfortable.

LIQUID-NITROGEN-FROZEN ICE CREAM

IT WASN'T THE RIGHT SEASON FOR IT, BUT so what? Smitten Ice Cream was definitely one of the best reasons I could think of to remain on this big, stupid scoop of a planet. They made it on-site, using some super-complicated piece of technology that had probably been invented when someone up at Stanford had been trying to find a way to cryogenically freeze the human brain. Instead they ended up developing the creamiest, most delicious ice cream of all time. The seasonal flavor was cinnamon apple crisp; it tasted like a Pop-Tart.

The plastic tables around the truck were filled up with San Francisco techsters, all silly mustaches and plaid shirts and phablets. In the last few years, these guys had pretty much taken over the city, turning wood and brick to glass and steel, forcing us natives farther and farther out, like one of those forest fires that sets all the animals running until they end up falling off a cliff. My mom always said San Francisco was a city of good intentions, but even if that was true, who gave a shit about intentions? What mattered were results. And the results here were not looking good. Half the city looked like an iPad, and the other half looked like a slum. The rich folks tooled around in their Tesla Roadsters and their Uber town cars, while stepping onto a public bus was like buying a ticket to the crazy museum.

We walked away from the packed tables and took a seat on the bars of this little metal dome that kids were meant to play on. Zelda dipped her pink spoon into the ice cream, then raised it to her perfect rosebud mouth. Lucky spoon.

"Mmm," she said, closing her eyes. "That's amazing."

Life-affirmingly amazing? I wrote in my journal.

She took another bite, savored, then slowly shook her head.

But this is the best ice cream on earth!

"That is arguable, Parker Santé. But even if it were, you're forgetting that I've been alive for two and a half centuries. I've eaten a lot of ice cream."

Liquid-nitrogen-frozen ice cream?

"Well, admittedly no. But have you ever heard of the law of diminishing returns?"

I shook my head.

"It's a dictum of economics that says there will always be an eventual decrease in the marginal output of a production process as one aspect of the production is increased."

I shook my head again, though this time it was to try and wring some semblance of sense from what she'd just said.

"Think about it like this. Can you remember the first time you were in an airplane?"

Sure. We went to visit my mom's sister in Seattle. I was six years old, I think.

"Now tell me about the last time you were on a plane."

Last summer. Exact same trip. Which sucked, by the way. My aunt is a bitch.

"Well, I can't comment on that. But the odds are good that that first plane ride was pretty exciting. You were thirty-five thousand feet in the air, looking down on the clouds, and you managed to survive, right? That's amazing! But I bet the last time you were on a plane, you weren't remotely amazed. In fact, you were probably actively annoyed about having to sit still for hours on end and eat a bunch of mediocre food. That's the law of diminishing returns. You always need a little bit more to reach the same high. It's the fly in the ointment of immortality."

God damn that was depressing. And hadn't I been thinking the same thing just last night, remembering how awesome Halloween had been when I was younger, and how lame it was now?

It's no different for non-immortal people, I wrote.

"Sure it is."

I don't think so. Like, take my dad. His most successful book was his first one. And my mom hasn't remarried because she doesn't think she could ever love anyone as much as she loved my dad. And it's true for me, too. When I was in elementary school, I loved going to school. I was seriously psyched to learn shit. Now I can barely stay awake through second period. I've just done it all too many times.

"Huh," Zelda said, "maybe you're right."

We finished our ice cream, which now seemed to get a little less delicious with each bite. Zelda sucked on her fingers. "So what's our next activity, Mr. I'm-going-to-convince-you-to-live?"

Shit. I hadn't actually thought beyond my ice cream gambit.

I'll tell you when I get back from the bathroom, I wrote.

"I'll be waiting."

As soon as I was out of Zelda's line of sight, I took out my phone.

Hey, Alana, I typed, *I need your help. I'm looking for shit to do with Zelda. Like, romantic shit.*

I was lucky; Alana started typing a response only a few seconds later.

You guys are still hanging out? Must've been a good night. You wanna share the details? Or maybe some pics?

I'm in a hurry.

Sorry. Take her to the Golden Gate Bridge. Gets 'em every time.

I don't think that's going to work here. Long story. Next idea.

How about a museum? Zelda seemed like the artsy type. You ever been to the Legion of Honor?

No, but she probably has. I'm looking for something she hasn't done before.

Museums don't work that way, Santé. Great art rewards repeated viewings. It gets deeper every time, like that scotch she gave us. By the way, you think she has any more of that shit?

Was Alana right? Could art be the exception to the law of diminishing returns?

Gotta run, I texted. *I'll try the Legion. Thanks.*

No worries, player. Lemme know how it goes.

When I got back to the dome, Zelda was just pulling her phone out of her purse. I jogged over and plucked it out of her hand.

"You took forever," she said.

S-o-r-r-y, I finger spelled.

"And did you figure out where we're headed?"

M-u-s-e-u-m.

"Museum," she translated. "Hey, I'm getting pretty good at that, aren't I?"

With one hand, I gave her a thumbs-up. With the other, I casually slipped her phone—still set to "Do Not Disturb"—back into her purse.

PORTRAIT OF A LADY LOOKING AT A PORTRAIT

IT WAS ONLY A FIFTEEN-MINUTE CAB RIDE from Smitten to the museum, and Zelda was onto the plan within the first five.

"I love the Legion of Honor," she said, just as the car was turning up Divisadero. "They have this wonderful painting of Paolo and Francesca. Do you know them?"

I shook my head.

"Dante wrote about them. They were doomed to float around on the winds of the second circle of hell because they'd allowed themselves to be slaves to lust during their lives."

H-o-t, I finger spelled.

"Isn't it, though? Hey, what's the sign for lust, anyway?"

I made the sign: a line drawn downward from chin to chest.

"How tame. What about sex?"

I put the sign for the letter *x* at the top of my cheek and slid it toward my chin.

"God, that's so disappointing. Isn't there slang or something?"

There *was* a more visually descriptive sign for sex, though it corresponded to a slightly less appropriate word. I made peace signs with both hands, simulating a couple of bunny rabbits, then bashed them together over and over again.

Zelda laughed. "Well, *that's* to the point."

The car pulled to a stop in front of a dirty stone fountain. From afar, the museum looked Greek (or maybe Roman— honestly, I have no idea what the difference is), with big stone arches and columns everywhere. A few tourists stood at the edge of the property, taking photos of the far-off Golden Gate Bridge, which didn't look so much golden as rusty. We got out of the car and walked a long cement path that led under an archway and into a broad arcade. Dead center was a bronze sculpture that I actually recognized. It was that famous one, of the guy resting his head on his fist.

"*The Thinker*," Zelda said. "The original is in France, of course, but I suppose one casting is as good as another. I've always found it rather insipid."

He looks like somebody trying to solve all the world's problems while sitting on the toilet, I wrote in my journal.

Zelda laughed. "He does, doesn't he? And now I'll never be able to see it any other way. Thanks for that."

I tipped an imaginary cap.

Just inside the building, an old woman sat working the ticket desk. She had a flowered brooch pinned to her sweater, right next to her name tag: GLADYS.

"Are you two students?" she asked.

I looked to Zelda, but she'd buried her nose in some pamphlet describing the museum's current exhibit.

"Hello?" Gladys said. "Are you students?"

I nodded.

"That's a yes?"

I nodded again.

"Cat got your tongue?"

I nodded a third time.

Gladys frowned. "I don't have to let you in, you know, if civility is beyond your capabilities. This is a private museum."

I put my journal up on the desk and wrote: *I'm not being a dick. I can't physically speak.* Then I spun it around so Gladys could read it.

I saw annoyance and pity battling it out on her face. Annoyance won. "That's no excuse for being obscene. Eight dollars each, please."

Zelda threw yet another hundred down onto the counter and headed into the museum without looking back.

"That was hilarious," she said, once we were out of Gladys's earshot. "What did you write to her, anyway?" I showed Zelda the journal. She laughed loudly, drawing stares from a couple of humorless museumgoers. "You should get that printed on a T-shirt, so you can wear it around all day. Do people often respond to you like that?"

All the time.

"But you refuse to go back to speech therapy."

I shrugged.

"Curiouser and curiouser, Parker Santé. And you act like *I'm* the mysterious one."

We entered a small, brightly lit room. A few run-of-the-mill bronze sculptures were mounted here and there, but the focal point was the enormous organ up against the wall. It had two big panels on either side of the keyboard, both of which were as dense with buttons, levers, and switches as the cockpit of a jumbo jet.

"The Skinner organ," Zelda said. "It cost over a hundred thousand dollars to build, which would be more than a million dollars today. They bring a man to play it every weekend. In fact, he should be here any minute. You see up there?" She pointed at a section of the wall above the room's entrance. "That's canvas, painted to look like brick. All the pipes are hidden back there. Trompe l'oeil, it's called. A trick of the eye."

I never would've noticed if she hadn't pointed it out, but now I could see the whole panel shivering with the draft. Funny, Zelda really did seem to know a lot of stuff. Art and history. French and Spanish and who knew what other languages. All of it very much in keeping with the story I'd promised her I now believed. I felt my faithometer nudge up to 38 percent.

"Come on," Zelda said. "Let's check out the exhibit."

I always get crazy tired in museums. I don't know what it is. Something about the air, or the light, or maybe just all that ART, coming at you like machine-gun fire—*bam, bam, bam*—all those haloed saints and weeping Marys and bleeding Jeses (that's the plural of Jesus, right?) and yawn-inducing landscapes

135

and dead chickens. Not to mention all that fucking fruit. Seriously, what is the deal with the fruit? Who decided that the best subject for art was a bunch of grapes and a pomegranate in a silver bowl? That guy ought to be beaten to death with an unripe pear.

Usually the only thing that keeps me awake is all the nudity. Though not nearly as common as bowls of fruit, naked ladies tend to feature very prominently in your average museum. You've got your life-size marble sculptures of naked ladies, still somehow as white as a fresh bar of soap. You've got your oil paintings of naked ladies frolicking under waterfalls. You've got your blocky cubist naked ladies that you only know are naked ladies because the title is something like "Naked Lady Descending Stairs." I can still remember those middle-school field trips, where we'd be corralled into a conga line and ordered to follow some boring-ass tour guide from room to room, and how everyone would get all nervous and blushy around the naked ladies. I liked to hang back and touch the paintings when no one was looking. It was an early and important lesson in the limited capabilities of watchmen. I've stroked the stone thighs of some seriously ancient statues in my day, and nobody's even raised an eyebrow. Teachers and museum guards put on a big show—"Don't touch this or you'll get in trouble!"—but the truth is, they don't stand a chance against us. They're the 300, and we're the fucking Persians.

Anyway, I didn't want Zelda to know I wasn't a regular

museumite, so I did my best to overcome my fruit-bowl-inspired sleepiness and look attentive. The exhibit was focused on this guy named Georges Seurat, who painted pictures with tons of little dots, like pixels on a computer screen. I wandered around, glancing at every painting for a few seconds, then moving on to the next one. Meanwhile, Zelda had stopped to stare at this one painting for, like, five minutes, so eventually I went over to see what it was. *Study for a Sunday on La Grand Jatte*, it was called.

"I was present at one of his earliest exhibitions," she said. "Do you know him?"

I shook my head.

"The style is called pointillism. Seurat's idea was that instead of mixing paints on a palette to create the colors he wanted, he'd put all the colors down separately on the canvas, and let the eye of the viewer mix them up. See this grass here? If you look closely, you can see it's got all sorts of other colors besides green in it. Colors you wouldn't normally associate with grass. But it's still grass, right? Isn't that amazing?" She leaned in closer. "I find I can lose myself in the flecks, if I stare hard enough."

And so we stood there, staring, and as my eyes went out of focus, I started to see what she meant. The spaces between the pixels began to shiver, and the colors pulsated and fused. I closed my eyes and could still see them there. A dog made up of purples and reds and greens cavorted against the black background of my eyelids. Trippy.

We walked on. The museum only had a few of Seurat's actual paintings; the rest of the exhibit was made up of the work of other people who did similar stuff in the years before and after Seurat, with bigger dots or smaller dots or differently shaped dots or whatever. So maybe it was true, that there was nothing new left to be done, nothing I could show Zelda that she hadn't already seen. But in spite of that disappointing revelation (and the fact that the work of the pointillists was woefully devoid of naked ladies), I was enjoying myself. Maybe it was because this was the first time I'd come to a museum voluntarily, as opposed to being compelled by an adult hell-bent on my intellectual betterment. I suddenly found myself really thinking about the paintings, in a way I never had before. Why had that painter over there gone to the trouble to put that bird in that tree, or that chubby cloud in that prismatic sky? Why was this fleck silver instead of brown? Every painting was made up of a million separate decisions.

The exhibition spat us out into a gift shop, where all kinds of random crap that had nothing to do with art was for sale. Zelda threw a colorful wool scarf around my neck and stepped back to observe.

"Gorgeous. You're getting it."

I checked the price tag: $250.00. This place was so classy, they didn't even bother writing it as $249.99. Zelda had bought the scarf before I could mount an argument against it. The wad of cash shrank yet again.

Afterward, we ordered coffee at the museum café and watched people watching the art. Nearly everyone was caught up in the business of reproduction: "serious" photographers with telescopic lenses on their schmancy cameras; art students sitting cross-legged on benches and sketching rough outlines on tracing paper; the professional tourists, with their blinking sea of smartphones held up like lighters during a metal band's power ballad.

Why do they all do that? I wrote.

"Do what?"

Take photos. Don't they know there are already tons on the Internet? Why not just look at the art?

"Beats me, Parker. People are so stupid, it's a wonder they manage to keep breathing."

I laughed. That was a good line; I'd have to use it in a story sometime. Which made me remember a thought I'd had while walking around the exhibit.

Do you think you could do pointillism in writing?

Zelda frowned. "I don't know. What would that be like?"

I guess you'd just use words. Single words. And try to tell a story.

"So today would be . . . what?"

I thought about it. *Wake. Diary. Breakfast.*

"Mother."

Tea. Believe.

For a nanosecond, I thought about writing down the *L* word.

And so on, I wrote instead.

"It could work, I guess. But it's basically just poetry."

Oh yeah. It is, isn't it?

At that moment, the music of the organ began to echo through the museum. It sounded like an entire orchestra.

So did this work? I wrote.

"Work how?"

Has all this beautiful shit convinced you not to jump off a bridge?

Zelda laughed. "Well, it certainly is a lot of 'beautiful shit.' But I've been to the Louvre, Parker. I've been to the Prado and the Whitney and the Met and the Frick and every other museum under the sun. So this was hardly going to be the straw that fixed the camel's broken back."

So how can I convince you?

"Parker, I . . ." She raised my hand to her lips and kissed it. "I think it's very sweet you're trying so hard. But I've begun to notice a worrying disparity in the care you show me and the care you show yourself."

What do you mean?

"I mean that you're putting all this effort into making me want to live, and yet you seem to put very little effort into your own happiness."

I knew what she was getting at, but it felt good to be worrying about someone else for a change, instead of just obsessing about my own bullshit like I usually did.

My happiness depends on you being alive.

"You can't predicate your happiness on someone else's happiness. That way lies madness."

So what am I supposed to do?

"For a start? Maybe stop showing me things you think I want to see, and show me things you'd want to see. What makes Parker Santé the happiest?"

That was a tough one. What *did* make me happy? There had to be something, but when I thought about what my life had been just two days ago, before I'd met Zelda, it seemed like a happiness wasteland. I hated school, and parties, and dances, and people. The only things I really liked were unsharable.

I like to read. And to write. I like making up stories.

"Yes! Like the story you made up yesterday, about the most beautiful girl in the kingdom. I loved that. Why don't you write me another one?"

Right now?

"Why not? We've got time."

When she said that last sentence, she glanced at her phone, poised faceup on the table, like a viper that could strike at any moment.

Okay. What about?

"Love. Let's have a love story."

STORY #2:
THE BOY WHO
COULD SMELL DEATH

THERE ONCE WAS A BOY WHO COULD SMELL death—

INTERRUPTION #1

"THAT DOESN'T LOOK LIKE THE TITLE OF A love story," Zelda said.

I glared up at her.

"Fine, fine. I won't read over your shoulder. Your handwriting is abysmal, by the way. Don't they teach children cursive anymore?"

You want a story or not?

"Yes. Sorry. Please finish. I'll be quiet as a . . . well . . . as you."

STORY #2:
THE BOY WHO
COULD SMELL DEATH

THERE ONCE WAS A BOY WHO COULD SMELL death. He said that it smelled sweeter than you'd expect—a little like almonds. When he was a toddler, no one believed him. He would pass a stranger in the street and tug at his mother's skirt.

"That woman smells wike death," he'd say.

INTERRUPTION #2

"WIKE?" ZELDA SAID.

He's a little kid. He struggles with his l's.

"I see. Please continue."

I will.

STORY #2:
THE BOY WHO
COULD SMELL DEATH

"THAT WOMAN SMELLS WIKE DEATH," he'd say.

And his mother would slap him upside the head. "What a morbid little mind you have. Don't speak such nonsense."

Then, one Christmas Eve, at a large family gathering, the boy was sitting on his uncle's lap, listing all the things he wanted Santa to bring him.

"A stuffed horse, and some mittens, and a wooden sword . . ." He trailed off. Then he leaned forward and sniffed his uncle's neck. "Uncle," he exclaimed rapturously, as if he'd just opened the first present under the tree, "you smell wike death!"

Everyone in the room went quiet, and the boy was rushed up to his room without dessert. A week later the uncle's heart seized up while he was in bed with his wife. His last words were "That horrible boy cursed me."

The next day the uncle's widow stormed into her sister-in-law's house. "I'll have nothing more to do with you while that demon lives under your roof. He killed my husband."

"It's not his fault," the boy's mother said. "My brother was fat as Santa Claus himself. He ate half his weight in bacon every day."

"So you're saying it's merely a coincidence?" the widow exclaimed.

The boy, who had been standing at the top of the stairs this whole time, suddenly ran down into the kitchen. "I didn't kill your fat old husband!" he shouted. "I just smelled death on him. It smelled wike almonds."

His mother slapped him upside the head again. "Go back to bed, child!"

But the gossip mill began to do its ugly business, and soon the boy was notorious throughout the town. Adults avoided him, but the other children felt strangely drawn to him. They'd saunter up when he was on his own—outside weeding the garden, or buying milk at the market—and ask nonchalantly, "So you're the boy who can smell death, are you?" And the boy would nod, because he'd been taught never to lie. And then they would want to know: "Can you smell anything on me?" And he would say no, which was the truth, because their town was a safe one, and these were only children. Confronting the boy who could smell death became a sort of adolescent rite of passage, like going into the basement of the abandoned house up on Banker's Ridge and counting to a hundred.

There was one boy in particular, a handsome but mean-spirited child named Charles, who found it hilarious to harass the boy who could smell death. Again and again, he'd ask,

"Hey, freak, do you smell anything on me?" And when the boy who could smell death replied that he smelled nothing, Charles would say, "Well, I smell something on you: my fist!" And then he'd punch the boy who could smell death in the shoulder or the stomach or the nose and walk off laughing.

But one day, four long years after the death of his uncle, the boy who could smell death *did* smell something on Charles, and because he'd been taught never to lie (and maybe because he was a little angry after all those years of abuse), he said so. "You reek of almonds," he said. "I give you a week at the most." Everyone around gasped, because the boy who could smell death hadn't ever answered in this way, not in all the years they'd known him.

Though he pretended to laugh it off, Charles was scared to his very core. The next day he walked to school more carefully than ever, looking both ways before crossing the street, and when he finally made it under the eaves of the schoolhouse, he heaved a sigh of relief. The sound of that sigh was just enough to shiver loose a big slab of ice on the roof, and it caved in poor Charles's little skull.

INTERRUPTION #3

"WHERE'S THE LOVE STORY ALREADY?"
Zelda asked.

I'm getting there!

"Well, get there faster."

You know, you're pretty impatient for an immortal.

Zelda just glared at me.

STORY #2:
THE BOY WHO
COULD SMELL DEATH

SOON AFTER CHARLES'S UNTIMELY END, the boy who could smell death was run out of town; the locals simply refused to believe that he hadn't cursed Charles somehow, or else murdered him outright. The boy wandered alone for a long time, growing gaunt and haggard, eating whatever he could trap or steal or beg, until he came to a town where there lived a girl with silver hair and silver eyebrows and even fragile silver eyelashes. She was also an outcast, because of the way she looked, and when the two teenagers met, they both saw themselves in the other.

"You look famished," she said.

"I am famished."

"Go hide in the barn. I'll bring you something."

And so he did. And so she did. And when they were together in the barn and the boy's hunger had been satisfied, the silver-haired girl asked him how he came to be a poor wanderer, and he told her that he could smell death, and that it smelled like almonds, and that everyone who knew him believed that he carried death with him, like an illness, when really he just smelled it. They called him a demon.

"They call me that too," she said.

"Just because of your hair?"

"Yes."

"People are so stupid, it's a wonder they manage to keep breathing."

"I feel the same way."

They fell in love that very instant. Over the few apples the silver-haired girl had managed to steal from the larder, they shared their first kiss. The girl pulled away when she heard the boy sniff.

"What is it?" she asked.

"Nothing," he said.

But it wasn't nothing. He had smelled death on her, hidden beneath the tang of the apples and the fresh scent of her hair. It wasn't close yet, but it was coming. The boy resolved not to spend a single moment apart from her, because their time together was to be so short.

She ran away with him that very night, and they drifted across the countryside together. They made love under the stars, and feasted on nuts and berries, and bathed in cold, clear streams. Every day the smell of almonds grew stronger, until it was practically overwhelming. The end was near now. The girl could scarcely move but for the boy suddenly reaching out and hugging her to him, as if even one step away from him was a step too far.

"What is wrong with you?" she asked, though she didn't entirely mind all the attention.

"Nothing. Nothing at all."

Then one day they were bathing in one of those cold, clear streams, when suddenly a great brown bear appeared from between the trees on the bank. It was ragged and scrawny, a desperate hunger in its inky eyes. And though the boy had never been wrong about the smell before, he set himself to defend the silver-haired girl as best he could. With the sharp pointed spear he used for fishing, he attacked the great beast. He stabbed it once, and then twice, and then it closed the distance between them and gouged a great chunk out of the boy's stomach. He fell to the ground but continued to fight, slashing out with the stick again and again, until a lucky thrust skewered one of the bear's eyes. The creature roared in pain and ran back into the woods.

"No!" the silver-haired girl shouted, and collapsed by the boy's side. "My darling! My darling!" She dug her face into the boy's neck and wept great big salty tears, but they were nothing next to the thick gouts of blood that poured out of him, soaking the grass.

When she pulled away to look at him, she was surprised to find him smiling.

"Thank God," he said.

"How can you say that?" she asked. "You're dying!"

"I know," the boy said. "But I've realized that all this time, it was my own death I smelled. Now the almonds are gone, and that means you'll live a nice long life. Soon you'll find another boy, one who can only smell your sweet scent, and you'll be very happy together."

"I won't. If you die now, I'll kill myself."

The boy shook his head. "But you won't, dear girl." He tapped his nose. "I'd know."

And then he drew his last breath.

THREE'S A CROWD, OR COMPANY, OR A TRICYCLE OR SOMETHING

"THAT WAS A LOVE STORY?" ZELDA ASKED.

I think so, I wrote.

"But it was so sad. Why are all your stories so sad?"

Sad stories are the best ones. Everybody knows that.

Zelda sighed. "I suppose that's true. Anyway, I still liked it. You'll have to include that one in your applications."

My what?

"Your college applications."

I'll admit I'd kinda forgotten about that part of our agreement, and Zelda could tell. "Don't you even *think* of trying to weasel your way out of our d—"

"P-Funk!"

Everyone in the café swiveled their heads to look toward the entrance. Alana stood in the doorway, still wearing most of her costume from the party last night, including the plastic cutlass (in a belt around her waist) and the billowy white pants. At least she'd taken the stuffing out of her butt.

"I'm so glad I caught you," she said, taking a seat at our table. "Hey, Zelda."

"Hello," Zelda said. "It's Alana, right?"

"Alana, the Pirate Queen!" She picked up my coffee and drank the dregs. "Ew. It's cold."

What are you doing here? I wrote.

"Right. So listen, I realize you guys are on a super-romantic date, and I'm sorry about that, but I basically haven't slept since Thursday, and I really needed to talk to someone, so after you texted me that you were coming here, I just figured why not, you know? I mean, it's not like I caught you in the middle of doing it or something."

"Parker texted you?" Zelda asked.

"Yeah. He was looking for date spot recommendations. Isn't that sweet?" Alana grabbed hold of one of my cheeks and pinched it. "He's a gem, our Parker is." I swatted her hand away. "Besides, I haven't been to the Legion in forever. You know, I'd forgotten how many bowls of fruit they've got up in here."

I was just thinking that! I wrote.

"They're still lifes," Zelda said. "Usually it's either bowls of fruit or strung-up dead animals."

"Dead animals are called still lifes?" Alana said. "That's fucked up. They should be called still deads." Zelda and I both laughed. "And when they say 'still life,' do they mean, like, life that is *still*, as in *not moving*, or more like, 'Sure, this chicken is dead, but it's *still life*,' you know?"

"The first one," Zelda said.

"Well, either way, they're hella boring."

"Once upon a time, the idea of a still life was revolutionary. Before that, paintings were primarily focused around religious scenes. Still lifes opened up the possible subjects of art to include the natural world."

Was there anything Zelda didn't know everything about? The needle of the faithometer kept ticking upward.

Alana whistled. "Damn, Santé. Your girl is smart. See, I knew this was the right call. Come to the Legion, get some culture, then get some advice."

What advice? I wrote.

"Let's discuss it over lunch. You guys about ready to bounce?"

We were going to eat here.

"Are you kidding? You can't wine and dine this beautiful lady at the museum café, Santé!" She pinched my cheek again, harder this time. "Museum food is for dumb tourists. I got a way better place in mind."

Where?

"Lemme just finish this real quick." She reached over and drank the rest of Zelda's coffee. "Ew. Also cold. All right, let's do this. I'll lead the way." She drew her plastic sword and marched out of the café.

It wasn't like we had to follow her, of course. But it also wasn't like I had any better ideas.

BRAINWASH

"WHAT IS IT?" ZELDA ASKED.

"It's BrainWash," Alana said, "the only combination laundromat, diner, and concert venue in the known universe."

She was attempting to parallel park in a handicapped spot just outside the laundro-diner-venue. I pointed out the sign. "Doesn't matter. I've discovered I'm totally irresistible to cops. Seriously, I've never gotten a single ticket, and I can't drive for shit."

To punctuate the point, she drove up onto the sidewalk and then back down again, jostling the car in front of us and then tapping the one behind. Somehow, we still managed to be about a foot and a half from the curb when these maneuvers were completed.

The place looked like your standard diner, with the standard Formica counters and neon signage and steel tanks of what had to be shitty coffee. Alana recommended the breakfast burrito, so we ordered three of them, then sat down at a metal table right next to the smallest stage I'd ever seen. Through a doorway, I could make out the laundromat portion of the establishment, which was crammed with weekend washers dressed in their laundry-day best.

"So what did you want to talk to us about?" Zelda asked.

"Right. So here's the thing—" Alana's attention was suddenly drawn to Zelda's right hand, which was poised to unleash a cascade of sugar into her coffee. "Hold up. You don't drink it black?"

"Never."

"But isn't life already fake enough without watering it down with sugar?"

"Can something be watered down with sugar?"

Alana frowned. "Okay, that's true. But just take one sip before you put that crud in."

"I've had black coffee before."

"I know, I know. Humor me."

Zelda lowered her face to the rim of the mug and came up grimacing. "Yuck," she said.

"Exactly! See, coffee is *supposed* to taste bad. That's what makes it coffee."

"I prefer the illusion," Zelda said, and went ahead with her cream and sugar.

"To each her own." Alana took a big gulp from her own mug. "It is pretty gross, isn't it? Maybe you've got the right idea." She poured in a bit of cream. "Okay, so here's the deal. I realize this might seem out of nowhere, given that I barely know either of you, but all my other friends are part of the same fucking clique, so there's no way I can talk to them, and Zelda, you just seemed so mature and shit at the party last night, and you two look so happy together, I figured who better to ask, you know?" She took a breath, then another sip of the coffee. "That is much better, actually."

Your point? I wrote.

"I think Tyler is cheating on me."

"Who's Tyler?" Zelda asked.

"My boyfriend," Alana said.

"And why do you think he's cheating?"

"It's just little things. Like, sometimes he doesn't answer his phone, and when I ask him where he was, he gets all nervous. And last night, at the party, he was really weird and distant and shit. Also, he works at this movie theater on the weekends, but he never wants me to visit him there. Oh, and then there was this one time where he had a hickey on his neck and it was really faint and he swore I was the one who gave it to him but I couldn't remember doing it."

"That's a lot of circumstantial evidence," Zelda said. "Do you have any hard proof?"

"Not really. Just feelings. Bad feelings."

"Interesting," Zelda said, and I could tell she really meant it. *Treat me exactly like a teenager,* she'd said to me yesterday. Well, nothing was more teenagery than relationship drama.

"Parker, what do you think?" Alana asked.

I'd never really liked Tyler, even though he was a lot nicer than Jamie, but maybe that was just because I was a little jealous of him.

159

I don't know, I wrote. *How could I?*

"Use your gut, man."

My gut just says I'm hungry.

"Parker's right," Zelda said. "You can drive yourself crazy with suspicions, but it doesn't do a bit of good in the end."

"Maybe. But I swear if he's cheating, I'm gonna cut his balls right off. He was my first, you know. That shit's no joke. Who was your first, Zelda? Some older man, I bet."

I knew that Zelda would lie, but I was surprised when she fed Alana the same lie she'd fed me. "Quite a bit older. His name was Karl. Sweet in his way, but a little severe."

Alana put out her fist for a bump. "That's the way to do it. Mature men for the win, am I right?" Zelda awkwardly returned the fist bump. "What about you, P. Diddy? Who was your first?"

Luckily, my burrito arrived at just that moment, and it was roughly the size of my head, so I was able to stall by taking one of the largest bites ever taken in human history. It was the second time that question had come up today, and though I hadn't minded telling Zelda the truth, it was different with Alana. She went to my school, and so had the power to spread the word of my virginity far and wide. I held up a finger—*Hold on while I chew*—and tried to figure out what I was going to say.

"I think Parker is worried about kissing and telling," Zelda said, coming to my rescue. "But I really don't care who knows. I was his first. First and only."

Weirdly, even though it wasn't true, just the saying of it made it real in some way, almost as if she were promising me something.

"Respect, Santé," Alana said. "I'm all about saving it for the good ones. If only they would stay good." She gestured with her burrito, sending beans and rice flying across the table. "By the way, you probably know this already, Zelda, but you're some kind of miracle worker. You're like *the* Miracle Worker."

"What do you mean?"

"I mean you've saved this boy's *life*, girl! Last night was the first time I've seen him out since the beginning of high school. It's like he actively hates being around other human beings. Right after every class is over, he's out the door. He doesn't even come to lunch."

I come to lunch, I wrote. *I just eat it in the library.*

"Whatever, man. The point is, nobody ever sees you. And it's not because anyone has a problem with you or anything, the way you seem to think they do. You're just never there— not even when you are. What's up with that?"

I looked to Zelda to save me again, but this time she seemed just as interested in my answer as Alana was.

I don't know, I wrote. *I just figured nobody wanted me around.*

"Why? Because you can't talk? No offense, but that's fucking stupid. Everybody hangs out with Jamie, and he's a total dick. We all *wish* that guy wouldn't talk. And Erik Jones spends every single party burping out Katy Perry songs and then throwing up in the bathroom, but nobody has a problem with him. You're cool, Santé. You're smart and shit. Even if you suck ass at chess."

I wasn't used to hearing people say nice things about me. I felt like I should be smiling, but I'd lost control over my face.

Thanks, I wrote.

"Hey, I just got an incredible idea!" Alana said.

"What's that?" Zelda asked.

"How about you guys go to the movie theater where Tyler works? You could check to see if there's any funny business going on."

I'm not sure that's smart.

"It *is*, though," Alana said. "I just said so. 'An incredible idea,' is how I described it. Did you miss that?"

I was readying more objections when Zelda piped in. "We'll do it."

"Really? You're the best!" Alana hugged Zelda across the table. "This is gonna be so much fun. You'll be like superspies."

We finished our burritos and paid up, but before we left BrainWash, Alana insisted we check out the laundromat.

"It's, like, the weirdest place ever," she said.

We followed her through the doorway and into the pungent funk of cleaning agents and damp fabric. There was a kind of loud silence, as all ambient sound was buried beneath the hot hum of the spinning dryers and the tidal *sploosh* of wet balls of clothes turning over again and again in the washing machines.

162

They were the square kind with round windows in the front, so if you stood back, you could almost imagine you were looking into the windows of an apartment building, the residents of which came in three varieties: swirly and sudsy, sopping and still, or away on vacation.

"One time, I lost an entire hour staring at these things," Alana said. "They hypnotize you."

"It looks rather cozy in there," Zelda said. "Like a bunch of little Jacuzzis."

We stood in a row in front of the machines, watching them spin. Around and around, like the moon orbiting the earth. Like the earth orbiting the sun. My mind wandered back to what Zelda had said a few minutes ago: *I was his first.* Was that just another float in her unending Macy's Thanksgiving Day Parade of fibs and fabrications, or a statement of intent? Would tonight be different from last night? And why did that thought make me feel at least as anxious as excited?

"Your hand's sweaty," Zelda said.

I hadn't even noticed she'd grabbed hold of it.

"All right, kids," Alana said. "Duty calls. Let's make like a couple practicing the rhythm method and pull on out of here."

WHAT YOU DO AT A MOVIE THEATER, PART II: THE RECKONING

FIRST OFF, YOU ORDER THE TICKETS ON your phone, so you can bypass the ticket office without being seen. It's a weekend, so the theater is busy enough for you to hide in the crowd. The venue is one of those massive cinema complexes with multiple floors, multiple little video-game arcades, and multiple snack counters. You find Tyler on the very top floor. He's shoveling popcorn into bags and dousing each one with "butter." He's joined there by three other theater employees. One of them has an acne situation that has already colonized his face and neck and appears to have designs on his torso. Another is so overweight that everyone else has to turn to the side to pass her in the narrow alley behind the counter. And the third is an undeniably cute girl. She's got pink pigtails and wears a lot of green sparkly eye shadow.

You stand at the back of the room and observe. Nothing happens for fifteen or twenty minutes, and then the lobby starts to empty out and you have to retreat to one of the arcades to wait. After another half hour or so (during which you demolish Zelda at a game of air hockey), the room begins to fill up again, so you head back out to the lobby to continue your surveillance. Tyler and the pink-pigtails girl are standing at opposite ends of the counter, but as they converge on the center to deliver a cardboard box of cheese-soaked nachos and an oversize carton of Milk Duds to a man who definitely doesn't need either one, there's a look. It only lasts for a second, but both you and Zelda recognize that sort of look, and you give each other a look to communicate the fact that you saw the look and that you both recognize the look. You're not actually sure *how* you recognize the look, because it isn't a look you can remember giving or receiving yourself, but some animal part of you, the same part that senses whether the dog on the chain outside the Starbucks is the kind that will snap at you if you get too close, the same part that can tell whether those dudes coming down the street are worth crossing to the other side for, knows that this look means, *We are totally engaging in some kind of sexual activities when we are not in front of people and serving nachos and Milk Duds.*

You take your time leaving the theater, because you know Alana will be waiting just outside, and the news you bring her is not good news. When you get there, she hurries across the street to you, and you give her a look that tells her about the look you saw, and she gives you a look that at first you think is going to be the precursor to a sobfest, but then you realize it's a look that's like *Oh* hell *no!* And then she's marching back across the street and you're chasing after her.

"Ticket?" the ticket-taker guy says. Alana stalks right past him. He turns and calls out after her. "Ticket? Your ticket?" His training has not prepared him for this level of insubordination, and you can see he is torn between his responsibility to chase after her and his responsibility to continue taking tickets. A few seconds later she has disappeared over the lip of the escalator. The ticket-taker guy shrugs.

"Oh well," he says, then turns to you and Zelda. "Tickets?"

You present your stubs and are waved through.

Alana has stopped on the first floor and is peering through the crowd to see who's working the snack counter. Zelda puts a hand on her shoulder.

"You're not thinking straight, darling. You need to calm down."

"Oh, I'm thinking straight as a fucking arrow," Alana says. "I'm thinking straight as a frat boy. Now where is that sleazy little shit?"

"Let's just have a nice sit-down, shall we?"

"Won't tell me? Fine. I'll find him without your help." She marches up to the counter, bypassing the line, and slams her hand down on the glass. Salt crystals hop up into the air like a colony of tiny insects trying to fly. "Where is Tyler Siegel?" she asks.

The girl working the register is unruffled by this sudden interruption; she doesn't even pause in handing over change to a customer. "Third floor," she says. "And you didn't hear it from me."

"Thank you."

Now you're on the move again, heading back up the escalator. Alana is knocking shoulders with half the people on it, and you follow after her, apologizing to each person in turn. You reach the third floor, hoping Tyler might have escaped to the break room. But no, he's still there. And it's shit luck for him, because he's just made some joke to the girl with the pink pigtails, and she's laughing way too hard, and it's like the good Lord put a target on his forehead.

"Douche bag!" Alana announces, loudly enough to silence all nearby conversation, particularly among those families here to see the kind of movie in which such language will definitely not be used. Alana—still dressed as a pirate—clambers over the counter like that evil Japanese ghost in *The Ring*, knocking over the child-size popcorn of some little kid, who starts to cry. The pink-pigtailed girl knows something crazy is going on, but she doesn't yet understand it has anything to do with her. Not until Alana has grabbed Tyler by his black button-down shirt and pushed him hard into the Icee machine, which begins to stream cherry-red Icee onto the counter.

"Baby," Tyler says, just before he's slapped hard enough across the face to earn an admiring chorus of "ooooohs" from the crowd.

"Get off him!" the pink-pigtailed girl shouts, and pulls Alana away from Tyler. And now the two girls have grabbed hold of each other's hair, yanking this way and that, screaming warrior screams of anger-pain. Tyler is just watching, unsure what his role here is, and you know you've got to do something.

You climb across the counter and try to get between the two girls, only they're locked up tight. You scoot around behind Alana and grab her waist, pulling her backward. Zelda is next to you, trying to defuse the whole situation with words. It is at this moment that Tyler seems to wake up, and now he's coming over to help, but the girls twist violently around, slipping in the cherry Icee that is now all over the tile floor, and you're tossed hard right at him, your elbow going straight into his stomach. He straightens up with a wince, and this is the moment you would explain that it was just an accident, if you could talk. But you can't talk, can you?

The shock comes first. It's not pain so much as blunt force. A faraway part of you registers that you've just been punched in the face, but there's no narrative yet. Nobody has been assigned the role of puncher: there's only the punch. And it comes with a bright light, just like people talk about, only it's not stars—more like a single bright white flash, a gunshot going off inside your head. Then you're moving backward and downward, toward the sopping-sticky tile. You land with a squish. That's when the pain starts, radiating outward from your cheek in hot waves. Blood is already dripping from your nose, an impossibly bright streak of red when you wipe it off on your arm, as if something truly vital were seeping out of you. Or that could be cherry Icee—it's pretty hard to tell right now. For the first time, it occurs to you to look up. And there's Tyler, face looming above you like the frozen scowl of a totem pole, shaking the bruise out of his knuckles. You see cherry-red rage, and you're only seconds away from jumping back up to your feet and ripping out his throat when you notice that Zelda has managed to slip around behind him, and then she slams his head into the glass wall of the popcorn popper, which shatters. And now it's all five of you down there in a dog pile behind the snack counter of the multiplex, and there's blood and Icee everywhere, and the wrestling match goes on for another minute or so before enough adults with name tags and serious expressions show up to pull you apart, and you're all dragged roughly through a door and into a small office.

And that's what you do at a goddamn movie theater.

AN ARRANGEMENT

THE MANAGER OF THE MULTIPLEX WAS A chubby guy with a terrible comb-over and a weirdly high-pitched voice. His name tag said PIREZ.

"I'll have to call the police, you know," he said. "That's the rule when there's a violent altercation. And property damage."

"Mr. Pirez?" Zelda said.

"And of course they'll be informing your parents, who will be responsible for paying for those damages, but God only knows if they'll actually pony up."

"Mr. Pirez?"

"And on a personal level," the manager went on, "I just hope you know how damaging this kind of behavior is. I don't have a lot of job security, and when things like this happen, everything gets blamed on me, which hardly seems fair—"

"Mr. Pirez," Zelda said, a little more loudly this time.

"What?"

"I was only going to ask how much damage you think we did."

"I really couldn't say."

"Estimate, if you would."

"Well, that popcorn popper's gonna be at least a few hundred to fix. And I had to give free passes to everyone who witnessed that—that *brawl*. And then there are the cleaning fees, of course."

"Would six hundred dollars cover it?"

"Well, uh, that's hard to say—"

"Let's say seven." Zelda opened up her purse and removed the wad.

"Damn," Tyler said, impressed.

Zelda counted out the bills. "One, two, three, four, five, six, and seven." She handed them to Pirez. "That's that. Now, may we be excused?"

The manager looked flummoxed. I'm sure he didn't want to get the police involved any more than the rest of us did, but the alternative here was being bought off by a teenage girl.

"I still have to call your parents," he said. "I can't just let you loose to start fighting all over again."

Zelda sighed theatrically. "Very well. But my parents are both dead, so I'm afraid you're out of luck with me."

"Really?" the manager said. "So who's your guardian?"

"I guard myself. Now please get on with it."

So the manager called up our parents one by one. And while he was able to get someone on the line for Alana, Tyler, and the pink-pigtailed girl, my mom proved unreachable.

"What about your dad?" Pirez asked.

"His father is also dead," Zelda said.

"Oh yeah? Isn't that convenient."

"No," Zelda answered, stone-faced. "Quite the opposite."

So Pirez called my mom back and left a message. Then we all just sat there, in silence, waiting. The manager occasionally left the office to do his job, but he never stayed away for long enough to make running away a viable option. I had Kleenex stuck up my nose to stanch the bleeding, Tyler was holding a washcloth to where the popcorn popper had sliced open his forehead, and both Alana and the pink-pigtailed girl had scratches on their cheeks and fork-in-a-toaster hair. Only Zelda had come out of the melee relatively unscathed.

S-o-r-r-y, I signed to her.

"Don't be," she said, and smiled. "I can't remember the last time I was involved in an honest-to-goodness fight."

An hour later the pink-pigtailed girl got picked up by a mother who also happened to be wearing way too much green eye shadow. Alana went next, escorted out by an older sister who clearly didn't give half a shit about what had happened.

"You drove yourself, right?" she asked Alana.

"Yep."

"Cool. I'll meet you at home."

A few wordless minutes after Alana left, Tyler coughed in a preparatory sort of way. "Hey, Parker," he said. "I'm sorry I punched you."

"I'm not sorry I put your head through the popcorn popper," Zelda said.

I-t-s o-k, I finger spelled.

"What did he say?" Tyler asked.

"He said it's okay," Zelda translated. "Because he's a very generous boy."

"Oh. Cool. Thanks, man."

Tyler's mom was a tiny little blond woman who didn't look capable of getting angry with anyone about anything.

"What happened?" she asked, then peeled the washcloth off her son's forehead to get a look at the cut. "This is deep," she said to Pirez. "He probably needs stitches."

"Not my job," Pirez said. "And your son is fired, by the way."

Finally it was down to just Zelda and me. Pirez checked his watch. "Jesus," he said. Time passed. He checked it again. "Jesus," he said again. Time passed. He checked it again.

"Excuse me, sir," Zelda said. "I don't mean to speak out of turn, but perhaps there's a mutually advantageous end to this story."

"What do you mean?"

"Well, you've left a message for Parker's mother, so she'll certainly find out about what happened here today. Maybe it's time you let us go."

"I'm not sure I can do that. I'm a parent myself, you know."

"Then perhaps you were a little bit conservative with your estimate of the damages to your property. Say by two hundred dollars or so?"

"Yeah," Pirez said, smiling a little. "Yeah, that sounds about right."

A few minutes later we were released back onto the San Francisco streets. Zelda was $900 poorer, and apparently I was starting to develop a pretty serious black eye.

"It's turning the same color as that sunset," Zelda told me, pointing out where the blue sky was bruising with nightfall. And I started to laugh, because it was funny how good that black eye suddenly felt, in spite of how much it hurt. It felt like living.

We walked for a while, back in the general direction of my house, enjoying the squeaky San Francisco trolley-car symphony. Fifteen minutes later, my phone rang.

"Get home now," my mom said, then immediately hung up.

DINNERTIME DEBACLE

ZELDA HADN'T WANTED TO COME WITH ME.
She told me she had enough experience with parents and kids to know that she'd be walking into a firefight. But I insisted. At this stage, I couldn't afford to leave her alone with her phone; she *must* have been wondering why that call from the hospital hadn't come in yet, and it wouldn't take long for her to notice the little "Do Not Disturb" symbol in the corner of her home screen. I had to provide nonstop entertainment, even if that entertainment involved my getting torn a new one by my mom.

She was standing in the kitchen when we came in, holding a mostly empty glass of wine. Her eyes were already rimmed with red.

"Hello, Zelda," she said.

"Hello, Ms. Santé."

"Thank you for escorting my son home, but I'd like to speak to him alone."

No, I signed. *She's staying.*

"Excuse me?"

She's staying.

My mom took a moment to absorb this, then laughed one of those little joyless laughs that are a parent's way of saying, *Oh, is* that *what you think is going to happen?*

"Fine. What do I care?" She refilled her wineglass. "So you got in a fight today. At a movie theater. Care to explain?"

I was helping a friend, I signed.

Another fake laugh, only this time it meant, *Oh, is* that *what you're going to say happened?*

"I don't see how putting a boy's head through a popcorn popper could possibly be helping anyone."

"Actually, I was the one who put the boy's head through the popcorn popper," Zelda said.

My mom turned her death glare away from me for a moment. "Zelda, has Parker told you that this wasn't his first fight? Did you know that he spent most of middle school doing this kind of shit?"

"That's really neither here nor—"

"In eighth grade, some boy was making fun of him, so Parker shoved him into the street and a car ran over his leg. Broke it in three places. He could've been killed."

Okay. So you may remember I mentioned this in passing a while back (page 52, if you wanna check up on me), and I said I'd eventually give you the details. Well, here we are.

Even though everything my mom said was *technically* true, it also wasn't the whole story. I hadn't tried to hurt anyone on purpose, and that kid—Trevor Jaffe was his

176

name—had been tormenting me all year. And it wasn't just "making fun of" me. He would push me too, and punch me, and trip me, and kick me—basically the whole bullying playbook. So yeah, I pushed him back *one time*, and I wasn't paying attention to where we were (waiting for the bus), and this one car was driving way too close to the sidewalk, and so yeah, he ended up getting hit. Trevor's parents pressed charges, and maybe because he was white and I wasn't, I got this minor version of assault put on my record. I was suspended from school for a month after that, and it ended up setting me back in all my classes, and in some ways I never really found my feet again. So there you go. That's the story. Do with it what you will.

"I don't know anything about the past, Ms. Santé," Zelda said. "But as for today, it really wasn't Parker's fault."

"I don't want to hear it. I really don't. This"—she pointed at me, then all around her—"has been my life for years now, ever since Marco passed away. It's been unending. Parker acts as if he's the only one who lost something. He gets to screw up over and over again and I'm supposed to hold everything together." Her eyes were filling with tears, the way they always did when she so much as mentioned my dad. "You have no idea how many excuses I've heard."

Zelda looked at me, as if asking my permission for something, though I didn't know what. (And if I had known, I probably wouldn't have given it.)

"And what's your excuse?" she said.

My mom was so sunk into her own emotional meltdown, she didn't fully register the question. "What?"

"I asked you what *your* excuse was."

"My excuse? For what?"

"For this show you're putting on. For the perpetual pity party you appear to be throwing yourself. Can't you see what a terrible example you're providing?"

"Young lady, you're in my house right now—"

"Exactly!" Zelda said. "And let's take a look at this house of yours, shall we?" She marched through the kitchen and on into the living room, to the photograph mounted over the television. It had been taken in Mexico, I think, or somewhere with a beach, anyway—my mom and my dad, looking a lot younger than I'd ever known them to be, a little younger than it seemed they ever could have been. Kids, basically. They were too close to the camera, which my dad was holding (a selfie before the age of the selfie), and smiling like the world was a deck full of aces. Perfect happiness.

"Look at that, Ms. Santé. Right in the middle of the room. And you wonder why your son is utterly arrested?"

"Because I have photographs of my late husband? What does that have to do with anything?"

"Parker could get better, but he doesn't want to. And that's because *you* could get better and *you* don't want to. You surround yourself with these so you won't ever let go, and that's what you've taught your son is normal. It's shameful, Ms. Santé. I'm sorry, but it's absolutely shameful."

"I will not stand here and be lectured about grief by a girl."

"But you expect your son to stand here and be lectured about self-control by an alcoholic?"

For the first time in the conversation, my mom was stunned into silence. In an instant, my mind flashed through a hundred different micro-memories: bottles piled up in the recycling bin, cranky mornings and sleepy evenings, the smell on her breath. They had a rule at Delta that you couldn't have anything to drink for twelve hours before a flight, and I knew my mom had never broken it. But I also knew that she made a *big* deal about not breaking it, and sometimes she'd pour herself a big Bloody Mary early in the morning, if she had an all-nighter coming up. Did that mean what Zelda said was true? And why hadn't I ever noticed?

Finally my mom found her voice again. "Get out," she said.

"With pleasure."

Zelda slammed the door behind her. In thirty seconds she'd stripped my mom of all parental authority. Now we were just two fucked-up people standing in a dirty kitchen with no idea what to say to each other. My mom lowered her wineglass to the counter with a shaky hand. I headed for the door.

"Where do you think you're going?"

Wherever she's going, I signed.

IN THE
SHAKESPEARE GARDEN

I RAN TO CATCH UP WITH ZELDA, AND together we walked north, back into Golden Gate Park. It was after eight, and the park was mostly empty, though there were still a few health nuts running the trails in their Lycra shirts and shorts, iPod shuffles stuck to their arms like multicolored Nicorette patches. Streetlights glowed orange on the major roads, but there was no light on the trail Zelda was taking, toward a locked gate and a metal sign that read SHAKESPEARE GARDEN.

"Come on," she said, and climbed over the gate.

I'd been in the Shakespeare Garden before, but it felt totally different in the dark, almost like a cemetery. A path ran between two rows of stone benches to a kind of altar, on which was posed a bust of the big man himself, with his balding head and his ruffled cravat and a look on his face like *Aren't I just the smartest fucker in the whole world?* I put my hand on his wide, naked forehead. It was cold to the touch.

"I'm sorry that had to happen," Zelda said. I figured that was about the biggest non-apology there was in the world, but it didn't matter, because I wasn't looking for an apology. In fact, I felt grateful for what had just gone down, though I wasn't completely sure why. "Your mother . . . it's like she has an ice cube in her mouth and she thinks she knows what it's like to freeze to death. Do you know how many people I've had to say goodbye to over the years?"

I realized Zelda was referring to her supposed immortality again.

"I was married right here," she said. "The second time, I mean. To Nathaniel. I had all sorts of fake documentation to make it, well, as legal as was possible. The only people here were his sister and the minister we'd hired. It rained all over my dress, but neither of us cared. It was silly to wear white anyway. Do you know why brides wear white?"

I nodded. We'd talked about that in the same Life Skills class where we learned why Super Mario owed a debt to the perpetually kidnapped Princess Peach. White was a sign of purity.

"I was very far from a virgin that night," Zelda said, then laughed. "But there were ways in which I felt like one. Which I realize sounds terribly sentimental, but so what? Some people just . . . renew you."

I had a thought, and it seemed important enough to merit writing down. It was dark in the garden, though, so I pulled out my phone and wrote it into a text message: *Maybe love is the exception to your whole law-of-diminishing-returns thing.*

Zelda took the phone and read it. "What a beautiful sentiment, Parker. I think I'd like that for an epitaph: Love is the exception to the law of diminishing returns." She started typing something, but it was a few seconds before I understood why, and by then, it was too late. "I'm sending this to myself," she said, and handed the phone back to me. Then she pulled her own phone out of her purse. She waited for the text to pop up, unaware that I'd sabotaged her connection. Bold action was required.

I moved across the dark distance between us and put my arms around her waist, pulling her into a kiss. I felt the clunk of her phone dropping to the grass. A moment later we were on the ground too. She rolled on top of me, pinning my arms behind my head, pushing against me in a way that made me forget every single problem I'd ever had or probably ever would have.

Then she stopped. She sat up on top of me like a little kid, her knees spread on either side of my hips.

"I didn't think I would want this, Parker. I haven't for a long time." She stared up at the sky, thoughtful in the starlight, and recited what I could tell was part of a poem. "'I feel that there is an angel inside me whom I am constantly shocking.'" She let her hands fall to my chest and stared me in the eye with a purpose that unnerved me. "Not here, though. Anywhere but here."

NO, YOU DON'T

AND SO WE RETURNED TO WHERE IT ALL began: the Palace Hotel. I'd never actually stayed there, of course, because the rooms were about four hundred bucks a night. Or eight hundred bucks a night, as it turned out, if you got a suite. Which we did.

"Let's have a drink first," Zelda said, and I got this electric feeling in my stomach at the thought of what that word "first" was referring to. "Have you ever been to the Maxfield? Actually, I believe it's called the Pied Piper now."

I shook my head.

"Then you're in for a treat."

The Pied Piper was an old-fashioned bar off the Palace lobby, all red leather armchairs and dark wood and bronze globes. Swanky-looking people sat around sipping red wine and whiskey from glasses that seemed way too big for the amount of liquid inside of them. That was something I'd noticed about the hotel restaurant, too—tiny amounts of food were always served on huge plates. It didn't make any sense. If you were going to serve people minuscule portions, wouldn't the smart move be to serve everything on minuscule plates, so that the food looked bigger by comparison? Whatever. Rich people were idiots. Give me a colossal BrainWash breakfast burrito any day of the week.

"I'll order," Zelda said. "I've got a pretty convincing fake driver's license. Plus, I'm the only one of us who can talk."

I sat down in one of the armchairs and watched her approach the bartender. She made a joke, and he laughed, and then he was mixing up two drinks for her. She never even had to get out the fake.

"Cheers," she said, returning with two glasses of scotch. We clinked and drank. It burned all the way from tongue to stomach, but I still nodded when Zelda let out an *ahh* of satisfaction and said, "That's smooth."

She crossed her legs and leaned back into the chair, swirling her drink like some kind of Bond villain. "So tell me, Parker Santé, what were you really doing here yesterday? Besides taking a long weekend, I mean."

I opened up my journal. *I like hotels.*

"Why?"

I don't know. They aren't part of real life, because nobody's here to stay. Also, nice hotels are always a safe place to steal, because everybody's rich.

Zelda laughed. "I'd almost forgotten about that! You took all my money!"

I brought it back.

"Eventually." Over the top of her giant glass, she scoped out the room. "Take something right now," she said.

I raised an eyebrow.

"Go ahead. I want to see you in action."

It was the work of thirty seconds. There was a coatrack just inside the entrance of the bar. I took a gray cashmere scarf and wrapped it theatrically around my neck, over the scarf Zelda had bought me back at the Legion of Honor. Then I reached into the pockets of a couple of coats until I came up with an antique silver lighter. I returned to my seat and presented it to Zelda.

"Bravo!" she said, applauding. We toasted again and drank off the rest of our scotch.

"I'll get us a refresher," Zelda said. "And I guess I won't be needing this." She threw her fake license onto my lap. Her age was listed as a just barely plausible twenty-two. Under hair color, it said *silver*.

It's funny, I wrote, after she returned with round two. *The thing that's fake about this ID is the exact opposite of what's fake about most fake IDs. You're pretending to be <u>younger</u> than you really are.*

She took the license back and looked at it. "I suppose that's true. But you want to hear a secret, Parker? No one ever really stops feeling young. We may get a job and a husband and a house, but the whole adulthood thing is just a charade. We're all pretending to have grown up. You know what the cruelest object ever invented is?" I shook my head. "The mirror. It breaks the illusion."

Not for you, though.

"What do you mean?"

You see the same thing every time, don't you?

I'll admit this question was a kind of challenge. My faithometer had been creeping up all day, but it was still shy of the critical 50 percent mark.

"Oh, that's just as bad, really, only in a different way. People don't like getting older, but they *do* like changing. Staying the same is a kind of death."

My mom told me once that she wouldn't be a kid again for a million bucks. She said things hurt more when you don't have any perspective on pain.

"That's true."

But doesn't everyone want to be young and hot forever?

"They only *think* they want it, Parker. But nobody really wants anything forever. Just for longer than they get it."

I want you forever.

She smiled, then leaned over and kissed me gently with her whiskey-sweet mouth. "No, you don't," she said. "But you want me tonight, don't you?"

I nodded.

"So finish your drink, darling, and let's go upstairs."

I did. Fire all the way down.

THE TRAGEDY OF THE MINIBAR

WE TOOK THE ELEVATOR UP TO THE TOP FLOOR.

"Once upon a time," Zelda said, "this place had big beautiful keys made of bronze. And now?" She held up the white plastic keycard and flicked it. "And so the whirligig of time brings in its revenges."

The electronic lock beeped, and we entered the suite.

Jesus H. Christ. This wasn't a hotel room. It was an apartment.

The decor looked like what your grandma would buy if someone gave her a million dollars and no rules. Every available square inch of flat surface had some pricey-looking tchotchke on it. In the living room, a glass tabletop rested on thick cement columns, with a vase of freshly cut roses and a silver bowl of fruit on top (*It's still life,* I thought). A couch upholstered in gold and brown lay like a muddy hippopotamus across an Oriental rug, facing the wide maw of a marble-edged fireplace. Shelves that wrapped all the way around the walls had been stocked with the sort of books that could have been film props: leather-bound, ancient, embossed with gold.

I went into the bathroom, which was covered floor to ceiling with tiny white tiles that glimmered like the inside of an oyster.

The tub was set in the middle of the room on a platform. All the faucets were a bright, shiny gold. I appraised myself in the mirror. My black eye was a rainbow radiating out from pink to dark green. I looked older than I had yesterday, and by a lot more than a day. Tomorrow I'd be a different person entirely.

When I came out again, Zelda was sitting cross-legged in front of the minibar, trying to unscrew the top of a tiny bottle of Maker's Mark.

"Oh, the tragedy of the minibar," she said. "Perennially overpriced and understocked. Besides, only alcoholics drink from little bottles like this." The *A* word made me feel a pang of remorse for my mom, on her own back at home. *Ignore it, Santé. Keep your head in the game.*

I took the bottle out of Zelda's hand and helped her to her feet. We faced each other, there in front of a massive four-poster bed. The only light was a golden streak from the cracked door of the bathroom. I kissed the line it cut down her face. Then we were on the bed, and she was taking off my shirt and I was taking off her shirt and that was enough for a while, to feel her warmth and to touch all the soft, dreamy places I'd dreamed about but never touched. And there was a part of me that was like, *Just this would be enough*, but there was another part of me that was like, *Hell no it wouldn't.* Zelda helped me resolve the conflict by unclasping my belt and pulling my jeans off. It made for a funny pause when she took off my socks (let's face it, there is nothing remotely sexy about socks), which was good, because it gave us both the chance to laugh. Then I shimmied her jeans (which were technically *my* jeans) past her feet and we got under the covers in just our underwear. We kissed for a while, in a way that made it feel like things were escalating even though we were still just kissing. Then she hooked her thumbs into the waistband of my underwear and began to tug them downward. . . .

I grabbed hold of her wrists.

"What's wrong?" she asked.

I didn't even know myself at first. But when she tried to kiss me again, I pulled away.

"Parker?"

I reached over to the bedside table for my journal.

If we're going to do this, I wrote, *I have to know who you are. For real.*

"You know who I am," she said quietly.

I don't, though.

"Yes, you do. You promised to believe me."

That's not how belief works. You can't force it.

"Fine!" Zelda said. "So let's say I've been lying to you ever since I met you, even though it's not true. Why would that matter? We're here. You're here and I'm here and we're in bed together. What more do you want? What will ever be enough to make you shut up and live your life?"

It was probably the two glasses of scotch that pushed me over the edge. But after everything we'd been through that day, and in light of everything we were about to do, the idea that she would keep lying to me just about broke my heart.

I'll tell you what would be enough. One second of the truth.

"And what's the truth, Parker?"

I gave her my best guess, based on the little evidence I had. *You're a normal seventeen-year-old girl, but someone you care about is very sick, and you don't know how to deal with it, so you made up this story.*

Zelda was up out of bed even before I'd finished, staring down at me with a palpable fury. "How do you know about that?"

So it's true, I wrote in big letters, so she could read them from where she was standing.

"How do you know about Nathaniel?"

I could have said it was just a lucky guess; maybe she would've even believed me. But I wanted an end to *all* the lies, not just hers.

Last night the hospital called. You were asleep when the message came in, so I erased it. And then I made it so your phone wouldn't get any more calls.

"You asshole," she whispered.

I kept on writing, trying to explain, but she was already getting dressed.

I was scared you really meant what you'd said about the bridge. I couldn't just stand by and let that happen.

She refused to look at what I'd written, no matter how much I ran around the room trying to shove it into her line of sight. Finally I grabbed her shoulder, and she spun and delivered a stinging slap right to my bruised cheek. I was blind with pain for a few seconds, and by the time I recovered, she was gone.

HOSPITAL FOOD

LUCKILY, I WAS PRETTY SURE I KNEW WHERE she was going: the University of San Francisco Medical Center, back in the Sunset. I didn't have the money for a cab, but I caught the N Judah below Market Street and made it there in less than half an hour.

A homeless guy in a Yale sweatshirt was sitting just a few feet away from the sliding glass doors, smoking a cigarette directly underneath a NO SMOKING sign. He nodded to me when I passed.

And *pow!* Hospital smell like a sucker punch to the nostrils, sending me reeling back to the month I'd spent here after the accident. Mushy food on beige plastic trays. The perpetual beeps and boops of machines that kept people alive or made sure they were still alive or sometimes even brought them back to life. The doctor like some distant father who never stayed quite long enough. Nurses of all shapes and sizes—everything from the gum-smacking almost-teenager to the humorless schoolmarm, from the spheroidal cat lady who insisted on showing me pictures of her "furry darlings" to the hippie nurse with dreads who gave me a book called *The Power of Now*. All that daytime television, and the weird fascination I had with the Univision telenovela starring the twin sisters who hated each other but loved all the same men. My mother asleep in a couple of wobbly chairs pushed up front to front, whimpering in the darkness.

I fucking hate hospitals. Which is funny, actually, because they're a lot like hotels. Both places are populated mainly by people who aren't planning (or hoping) to spend a lot of time there. Both places have a ton of rooms with more or less the same shit in every one. Both places are constantly being cleaned but still somehow feel incredibly dirty. Of course, there is one important difference: nobody goes to a hotel because they're about to die.

The triage nurse looked up from her computer and noticed my epic black eye. She spoke with some kind of Caribbean accent. "You looking for the ER? That's a nasty one you got there."

I'd already prepared my question in the journal. *My name is Parker. I don't speak. I'm looking for Nathaniel Toth. He's a patient here.*

The nurse began to type into her computer. "Don't speak, huh? That some kind of religious thing?"

I shook my head.

"I got a kid married to a Jehovah's Witness. Man doesn't believe in blood transfusions. I say, 'You know how many lives I've seen saved because of blood transfusions? Every day, dozens of people.' But maybe I'll get up to heaven and the Lord'll tell me I can't come in because I had a blood transfusion once. Then won't I feel stupid?" She laughed loudly. "Here we go then. Nathaniel Toth. Seventh floor. Follow the signs for Geriatrics."

I shared the elevator with a doctor and a bald kid on a gurney. The kid gave me a big smile when I flashed him the peace sign.

It was past ten o'clock, so the ward wasn't exactly popping. In fact, no one was working the front desk at all. I walked the hallways, looking into every room. A lot of the patients were still awake, watching their ceiling-mounted televisions or reading some thick paperback. Their names were printed on labels just outside their rooms. It only took a couple minutes to find N. TOTH. I put my ear to the door but didn't hear anything, so I went inside.

It was a private room. An old man was sitting up in bed, but he wasn't awake, or else just didn't register my coming in. A plastic tube was sunk into his throat, and an IV was stuck into his arm. The EKG beeped.

On the bedside table, a small collection of framed photographs had been set up. First a young man with a young girl, posed romantically. Then a slightly older man with a young girl, still posed romantically. Then an even older man with a young girl, only now the pose was merely familiar.

Maybe it wasn't her in all those pictures. Different members of the same family can sometimes look pretty damn similar. My mom has this one photo of my great-grandfather up in the kitchen. He's eight years old, posed with his schoolmates. It was taken in Colombia, back in the 1920s or something, but the crazy thing is he looks *exactly* like I did at that age. My mom even taped up one of my own little class photos next to it, so you could see the resemblance.

But as I grew up, the physical similarities between me and my grandfather-as-a-boy had faded, whereas the girl here remained a dead ringer for Zelda in every photo. Always the same tiny mouth, the same silver hair, the same oceanic eyes. And who was this guy she was looking at like he was the best thing since the jelly doughnut? Could it really be the same old man who was lying in this bed? I stared at him, trying to find the parallels, but he was skeleton skinny and his face was a back-of-the-cereal-box maze of deep wrinkles. I needed to talk to him, to find out the truth once and for all. I touched his arm as gently as I could. Skin like tracing paper someone had spilled little pools of green and purple ink on. Nothing. I tried again, even shaking his shoulder a little bit.

"He's comatose," Zelda said. I jumped at the sound of her voice.

She shut the door behind her. In her hand, she held a wet washcloth. "I don't even know if he can feel this." She sat down at Nathaniel's side and began to dab at his forehead. "He started getting really sick at the beginning of the year, but we didn't move back to San Francisco until August. He wanted to be back in the place where he grew up." I stood totally still, not trying to sign or write anything, as if I could apologize for what had happened at the Palace by just shutting up and letting her talk. "I lost him for good a few days ago. They told me he'd probably slip away on his own. That was the phone call I was waiting for." She'd begun to cry, and though I wanted to reach out to comfort her, I held myself back. "But I just spoke to the doctor. It seems Nathaniel's stabilized. That was the message they left for me last night. He could stay like this for months before he goes. So now I'm supposed to decide when to—because I'm listed as his granddaughter and only surviving relative. Can you imagine?"

She dabbed at her eyes with the washcloth, then set it aside.

I felt my faithometer rushing forward. All these photographs of a girl who never seemed to age. 60 percent. The stubborn way she'd held to her story all day, no matter how many times I accused her of lying. 70 percent. Her encyclopedic knowledge of art and history and scotch, her maturity and sophistication. 80 percent. The stupid way she danced. 90 percent.

Zelda used her fingers to wipe the wet strands of silver hair off the old man's forehead, with a tenderness that was more than daughterly, and the last of my doubts melted away. Everything she'd told me was true. She'd been born two hundred and forty-six years ago in Germany, and the man in this bed was her husband, and when he died, an hour or a day or a year from now, she had every intention of jumping off the Golden Gate Bridge. And hadn't we read in biology class about a woman in France who lived to be 122? Zelda's story had never been strictly *impossible*—just really, really, *really* unlikely.

I believe you, I wrote in my journal.

"Good," Zelda said.

But now I've got about a million questions.

"Can they wait until morning? I think I should stay here tonight."

Okay.

"You can stay too, if you want. It's not very comfy, but I've slept in these chairs before, and it's survivable."

I pointed at Nathaniel and raised an eyebrow.

"He wouldn't mind. There's no jealousy between us. It's been years since we were . . . like that. He told me a million times I ought to find someone else. I just didn't see the point. I decided a long time ago that my life would end with his."

So I dragged a chair from the empty waiting room down the hall and set it up in front of the window, next to Zelda's. We sat facing the ocean, wrapped up in blankets, with our legs up on the sill. The valley below the hospital swirled with fog, like a bowl of dry ice. I was just nodding off when Zelda spoke.

"I'm sorry about before," she said. "I know why you did what you did. You were trying to save me."

My journal was across the room, so I put up a hand and slowly finger spelled my question.

W-h-y h-i-m?

196

"Why Nathaniel? As in why did I fall in love with him?" I nodded. "Oh, I don't know. Why does anyone fall in love with anyone? I don't believe we each have some single special person waiting for us out there, if that's what you're getting at. I've been in love too many times over the years to buy into that old canard. It's more a question of timing, you know? As if we all have these elaborate locks inside our hearts that are constantly changing shape, and every once in a while, someone happens along with the perfect key. Love is nothing more than a fortuitous collision of circumstances. And then you discover you've ended up spending fifty years with someone."

She reached under my thin blanket and squeezed my arm. "Now get some sleep, Parker Santé."

She got up and went back to sit at Nathaniel's bedside. I stared at the fog rolling off the water and listened to the beep of the EKG, picturing the peaks of Nathaniel's pulse, and I fell asleep imagining the interminable mountain range of Zelda's heartbeat, stretching back across the centuries and disappearing into the unknowable future.

SUNDAY, NOVEMBER

2

GOOD MORNING, SAN FRANCISCO

DON'T YOU HATE IT WHEN YOU HAVE A dream and it's totally obvious what it means? I've always preferred the super random ones—like where you're riding around some futuristic Tokyo on your hoverbike, but then you realize the hoverbike is a rhinoceros, except no, it's actually a *robot* rhinoceros being piloted by Prince, and he starts to sing "Purple Rain" as he flips a switch to activate the robo-rhino ejector seat, and you're launched up into the sky, watching as Prince's purple crushed-velvet suit and fluffy white cravat get smaller and smaller, and you should be falling by now but you're not, because you've become a balloon, and you just go on floating out into space until the world disappears and you can hardly breathe because of the lack of oxygen, and then you wake up and you're like: *What the fuck was that?*

But the dream I had that night in Nathaniel's hospital room was so easy to interpret it was almost embarrassing. I was chasing Zelda down these narrow city streets, and even though I've never been to Germany, I knew somehow that that's where we were. And even though Zelda didn't seem to be going very fast, I couldn't seem to catch up with her. My legs felt weak, and my heart was pounding like it was about to explode all over my rib cage. It wasn't until I caught sight of my reflection in a shop window that I understood why: I'd become an old man. The dream-past burst open in my mind, and all at once I remembered that Zelda and I had spent our entire lives together—or *my* life, technically—and now I was dying of some nameless illness and she was planning to kill herself, to jump off some Gothic German bridge into some icy German river. I would never catch up with her, but somehow I knew there was a way to make her stop running. So I hummed and hummed, the way Dr. Joondeph had taught me to all those years ago, and because it was a dream, a word came.

"Zelda!" I shouted. My voice was weak and quavery and ancient, but she'd heard it, and it had stopped her in her tracks. She turned around to look at me.

"Beep," she said.

"What?"

"Beep," she said again. "Beep. Beep."

Beep.

Beep.

I opened my eyes. The hospital. I tried to sit up, and my body immediately and painfully informed me that I'd just spent six and a half hours asleep in a poorly designed hospital chair. It felt like my bones had been replaced with gravel.

I emitted my silent version of a groan and managed to get to my feet. Zelda was gone, her blankets balled up on the chair next to mine. Nathaniel was just where he'd been last night, of course. I opened the shade. Mist lay thick over the Sunset, like a quilt pulled all the way up to the ocean, where it broke apart to reveal the sparkling water beneath. The sky was one enormous cloud. My mom said the air was always bumpier inside clouds, which was funny, because they looked so peaceful from the outside. They were a little like people that way. I wondered what kinda crazy shit was going on inside Nathaniel's head right now.

"Room service!"

Zelda arrived with two cups of coffee and an assortment of individually wrapped pastries on a tray. She placed it all on the windowsill, and we gazed out at the whiteness while we ate. "My God, my neck is killing me," she said, mouth half-full of cinnamon bun. "When I think of that beautiful suite we let go to waste last night, I almost want to cry."

I could have cried to think about what I'd missed last night too (and I'm not talking about the suite). I opened up my journal and noticed I was down to the last couple of pages; I'd done more writing in the past twenty-four hours than I usually did in a month.

So do I get to ask you all my questions now?

"Didn't you do that yesterday?"

I was just messing around yesterday. Now I actually—

I stopped myself midsentence, but it was already too late.

"Believe you," Zelda finished.

I nodded.

"Fine. Go ahead. What do you want to know?"

I asked the first question that had occurred to me last night, when my faithometer finally hit 100 percent.

Are there others like you?

"Do you mean others like me in terms of my general flair and joie de vivre? Or other immortals?" She waited a second, then spoke again before I could write anything. "Either way, the answer is no. Or not as far as I know, at any rate."

Isn't that lonely?

"Life is lonely. But less lonely for pretty teenage girls than for others. Next question."

So you lived through a lot of stuff.

"I did. Is that your question?"

No. I mean . . . hold on.

I tried to put myself in the shoes of one of my history teachers. How jealous would they have been to know I was talking to someone who'd seen all the shit they were always droning on about?

What was your favorite, like, time in history?

"Today," Zelda said.

No, I mean, when was the best time to be alive?

"Today."

Today? A random Sunday in November is the best time ever in history?

"Absolutely. In my opinion, the best time to be alive is always right now. People are always whining about how they were born in the wrong century, but they really haven't thought things through. They picture the old castle they wish they could live in, but they don't think about the drafts in the winter, or the pitch darkness at night, or all the spiders and the lice. They can't imagine the everyday pain of a life without antibiotics or anesthetics. The tedium of a world without movies or recorded music or . . . or . . . Internet videos about cats. And don't even get me started on *women* who idealize the past. Do you have any idea what it was like to be a woman even a hundred years ago? Horrible! And a hundred years before that, the situation practically defies description. We might as well have been slaves. Trussed up in hoop skirts and corsets, married off like racehorses. Good riddance to history, I say!"

Zelda turned her head and spat onto the tile floor.

"I probably shouldn't do that in a hospital," she said quietly.

Forget I asked, I wrote.

"I will."

So can you tell me the best place you've ever lived? Or is that question no good either?

"No, I like that one. Only there are so many good answers."

Paris? People always say Paris is the shit.

"Yes, I've never understood the American obsession with that city. The food is actually quite terrible on the whole, and the people can be rather awful if you don't speak the language. Of course, I first visited before Haussmann's redesign, back when it was just another dank medieval city, and I can't seem to get that image of it out of my head. No, I think my favorite city is still Berlin, in spite of all its flaws."

Where do you put San Francisco on your list?

"Above Zurich, but below Cape Town."

I have no idea what that means.

"Then you should travel more. Like Nathaniel and I did."

She looked over at her—it was still hard to think about him this way—husband. I realized there'd be time to ask Zelda more questions later. For now, I just wanted to get out of this hospital room.

Well, I could go on asking you stuff forever, but like you said, fuck history.

"I don't think that's exactly what I said."

Whatever. The point is let's go out and do something, yeah?

"Parker . . ." Zelda hesitated. "Parker, I think this has to be the end."

What?

She closed her eyes, as if she could find more resolve that way. "It's time for us to say goodbye."

MANDATORY PARTINGS

"I'VE HAD A LOVELY TIME WITH YOU," SHE said, still not looking at me. "Really I have. But it seems to me I should be on my own now, to figure out what I'm going to do about Nathaniel. Can you understand that?"

Sure, I wrote, though I didn't really mean it.

She opened her eyes again, exhaled. "Good. I'm glad."

We ate the rest of the meal in the beepy, respiratory silence of the hospital. I felt like someone getting kicked out of the house after a one-night stand, except this was worse, because Zelda and I hadn't even slept together. When the food was gone, I stood up and Zelda stood up and we hugged for a long time. I wanted to kiss her, but it felt weird to do it in front of Nathaniel, even if he *was* comatose.

"Goodbye, Parker," she said. "Thank you for the most fun I've had in a long time."

I made the sign for "goodbye," which I assumed she could understand from the context, and then the signs for "I love you," which I assumed she couldn't.

My steps sounded weirdly loud as I walked down the tiled corridor, away from Nathaniel's room. I didn't bother to wipe my eyes. If anybody saw me, they'd just assume someone I cared about was dying. And in a way, someone was.

If the elevator had taken me straight to the ground floor, that probably would've been the end of things between Zelda and me. But by some twist of fate, the doors opened on the fourth floor, and I saw the sign for the Center for the Deaf.

I haven't spent much time around deaf people, or not since back when my condition was first diagnosed, anyway. At twelve, I was still young enough that my mom could force me to go to these "mixers," where people with hearing impairments got together and played board games and practiced signing and making friends and stuff. I can still remember being surprised at how happy and normal everyone seemed. I mean, it wasn't like I'd expected all of them to stand around crying or something, but I also hadn't expected that the subject of having a disability would almost never come up. And the crazy thing is that I think I stopped going to those events *because* everyone seemed so well adjusted. All those happy, normal people made me feel even more like a fuckup, and I didn't want to bring everyone down with my fucked-up-ness.

It had been years since I'd been in a room made up primarily of deaf people, and I was curious to see what it was like. So I got off the elevator and found a seat in the waiting room. A little girl with cochlear implants was reading *Highlights*. An old man in a natty brown suit sat next to an old woman in a pink dress. Neither of them said anything—in sign or in speech—but they looked perfectly content doing nothing together. The only people signing were the couple in the corner. They had a stroller in front of them, and the baby boy inside it was looking around the room with your standard babyish curiosity, each glance asking some *super*-important baby question: *What the hell's that thing?!* or *Where the hell did my mom go?! (Oh, there she is)* or *Why the hell is that toy I just threw on the ground still on the ground?!*

I "listened" in to what the couple was saying. (As you can imagine, it's basically impossible to have a private conversation in sign.)

Tell them no. Say we're going to be exhausted, the woman signed.

They're my parents. They want to spend the holiday with their grandchild.

Well, they can't. There isn't space.

They can stay in a hotel.

And they'll be at our house ten hours a day.

So what?

The baby began to cry in an exploratory sort of way, like he was using the sound to measure the size of the room, or the size of his parents' love. They couldn't hear him, though, either because they were both deaf, or because they were too caught up in their argument, so after a minute, I crossed the room and knelt down in front of the stroller. I can't make any of the sounds that people usually make for babies, so I just twisted up my face into a monster scowl and offered the kid my finger. He stopped crying and grabbed on to it. I looked up at his parents, who had stopped arguing.

Cute kid, I signed, after gently recovering my finger.

You want him? the boy's father signed back, and his wife gave him a little fake punch in the shoulder.

How old?

Eighteen months, the mother signed.

He's here for surgery?

She nodded.

A nurse came out from the office behind the reception desk. *We're ready now,* she signed to the baby's parents.

We all stood up. The baby had given up crying, content now that the world had recognized his existence. I didn't leave right away, but stood in the doorway to watch the parents kiss their baby on the forehead and hand him over to the nurse. Though she'd seemed perfectly fine a minute ago, the baby's mother started to cry. After her son was gone, she turned and buried her face in the father's shoulder.

I've heard of people who like to hang out at the arrivals gate at the airport, because it's such a uniformly happy place. All these people reuniting with their loved ones, over and over again, 24-7-365. WELCOME HOME signs and little kids being lifted up into the air and deep, shameless kisses. Hospitals are basically the opposite of that. Everywhere around me, people were being forced apart by circumstance: illness and infirmity and death. Life would take everything from you eventually. So who would be so stupid as to leave someone they loved by choice?

I rode the elevator back up to the seventh floor. Zelda was still sitting at Nathaniel's side, watching some sitcom on mute. She didn't notice me come in until I reached up and turned the TV off.

"Parker, what are you doing?"

I sat down on the floor with my journal in front of me. *He doesn't need you anymore,* I wrote. *But I do.*

I watched a million possible responses flit across her face. She glanced down at Nathaniel.

"You'll look like him someday," she said. "I'm not going through it all again."

I'll never look like that. Colombian men age very gracefully.

Zelda laughed, and I could tell by the way she squeezed Nathaniel's arm that she'd made up her mind, at least for the moment.

"How terribly vain."

It's just the truth, I wrote.

"My, my. You've almost filled that whole notebook out, haven't you?"

I drew a smiley face in the last open corner.

"Do you have another one?"

I shook my head.

"Well, I still have some money left, and I've allowed this spiral-ring abomination to go on long enough. Let's go buy you a present, shall we?"

APPLY YOURSELF

"THIS IS A MOLESKINE," ZELDA SAID, HOLD-
ing up a large black notebook. "It's basically the most famous
paper product on the planet. Hemingway wrote in one of these.
Now, you will."

We were at FLAX on Market Street, just a half mile or so
from the Castro. It was one of those fancy art stores full of
colored paper and paint smell and hipster art students. I'd
always done all my journaling in the sort of notebooks you
can get for ninety-nine cents at Kmart. They worked just fine,
as far as I was concerned, but Zelda seemed excited to get me
something more "professional."

"We should buy a few of them, considering how quickly
you tear through the things."

We also picked out a couple of ultra-fancy pens. They were
as thick as my thumb, with shiny, diamond-shaped nibs and
leather cases.

"A good pen makes it look like you have better handwriting
than you really do," Zelda said. "It's a kind of cheating."

Altogether, the notebooks and pens cost more than three
hundred dollars. Zelda's wad of cash was now a sad shadow of its

former self—probably no more than six or seven hundred bucks left. When we were outside again, I uncapped one of the pens and wrote on the first page of a fresh journal. And straightaway, I saw that Zelda was right. My handwriting *did* look better.

Your money's almost gone.

"That's true."

We're going to have to be a little more careful from here on out. No more shopping sprees.

"Actually, I'm glad you brought that up," Zelda said. "I seem to remember that our agreement didn't simply involve my giving you loads of money for nothing. You were going to apply to college in exchange."

Not until the cash was gone.

"That's entirely unreasonable and you know it. I won't be able to check up on you to see if you go through with it. By that time, I'll be swimming with the fishes."

You said you wouldn't do that until you got the phone call.

"Which I did. Nathaniel's stable, Parker. I'm not just going to sit around waiting for him to die."

So now you're going to do it when the money's gone?

"Why not? It seems like a fitting ending."

Then I won't let you spend it.

"Oh, you dear boy. I don't need your permission to buy things. I could turn around and purchase fifty more notebooks right now. Shall I?" She took a step back toward FLAX, and I had to sprint to get between her and the door.

"Then we're agreed," she said. "You'll be applying to college forthwith."

But applications aren't due until the end of the year.

"So what? Haven't you ever finished an assignment early?"

No.

Zelda rolled her eyes. "Come on. We're awake and alert. We're young and beautiful. We've even got fresh paper and pens."

Well, if I hadn't believed her before, I definitely would have now: only an idiot or an immortal would think you needed paper and pens to fill out a college application in 2016.

It's all online now, I wrote. *We need a computer.*

"So where's a computer?"

At home, but I'm not going back there right now. Not after what happened between you and my mom.

"So find somewhere else."

I thought about it. *I guess I know a place.*

"You do? Then why are you scowling?"

Because I can't believe we're going to school on a Sunday.

A couple of years ago, my school had enacted a policy to keep the library computer lab open on weekends, so students could come in and do their homework there. Though I'd never gone myself, some kids from Chess & War had mentioned that they'd started going every weekend, so they could play online games together.

Zelda and I took the train back west and got off at the Twenty-Third Street stop, then walked the six blocks to my school.

"A bit brutalist, isn't it?" Zelda said.

I nodded. The campus was made up of a bunch of cube-shaped concrete buildings with these narrow little slits for windows—kinda like those holes in medieval castles that archers would shoot arrows out of. A parent volunteer sat on a plastic orange chair outside the library, reading a book called *How to Make Millions*. She looked up at us, tilted the bill of her 49ers cap to keep the glare out, and frowned.

"Student IDs."

"I'm his guest," Zelda said, after I'd presented my ID.

"No guests allowed. There's a lot of expensive computer stuff in there."

"I completely understand," Zelda said, then leaned in with a conspiratorial intimacy. "But I'm Parker's application adviser, and we absolutely have to start working today. Do you really want to be responsible for this little angel not getting into college?"

Zelda gestured toward me, and I gave my most angelic smile. The parent volunteer looked back and forth between us a few times, then let out an annoyed little grunt. "Fine," she said. "But I swear if we catch any more of you kids having sex in the basement, we're gonna shut this whole project down. Sign here, please." Zelda entered her name in the log, and we passed through the doors of the library.

The place smelled like books and boredom and unpopularity. A bronze sculpture of a monkey by the circulation desk was worn down on top where people had rubbed his head for good luck. Sure enough, half a dozen kids from Chess & War were already ensconced in the computer lab, blowing each other's heads off in Call of Duty. I sat down in the back row before anyone could notice us.

"What are they doing?" Zelda whispered, taking the chair next to mine.

Computer games, I wrote.

"Friends of yours?"

Not really. Don't worry about them.

"Okay. So . . . where do we start?"

How should I know? I've never applied to college before.

"Well, where do you want to go?"

My real answer would have been "nowhere," but I had to come up with something. *SF State,* I wrote, pulling the name out of the air.

"Why there?"

I don't know. It's close. It's not too selective.

"Those are incredibly stupid reasons. I think we can do better than that. Let's come at it logically. You want to write, yes?"

Sure.

"So who's your favorite writer?"

My dad, I wrote on instinct, even though it wasn't true.

"Other than him."

Ursula K. Le Guin, I guess.

"I've never heard of her."

216

She writes science fiction.

"Aha."

Zelda typed "Ursula K. Le Guin" into Google and hit the search button. She clicked through to the author's Wikipedia page and read her bio.

"Uh-oh," Zelda said.

What?

"I was hoping to see what school she went to, so you could apply there, but it turns out she went to Radcliffe."

You don't think I could get in?

Zelda laughed. "No, but only because it used to be an all-girls school, and now it doesn't exist. But look, it says here she went to Columbia for graduate school."

Where's Columbia?

"New York City. I've walked around the campus before. It's absolutely gorgeous. I'll show you."

She pulled up the Columbia website and we began to click through the photos. The place didn't look like a college so much as a European resort, with huge stone fortresses for buildings and all kinds of well-dressed, smart-looking kids walking around. Zelda found the page for the creative writing program, which talked about all the famous authors who'd studied there and all the famous authors who taught there. I had to admit, the whole thing looked pretty badass.

Then we found the page that explained what all this luxury cost.

Fuck, I wrote in my journal. Then I underlined it. Then I put it in a box with stars and dollar signs around it.

"They give scholarships," Zelda said.

Not for me. My GPA sucks.

"You're being negative. Today is not about being negative. Today is about being positive. And I am positive that if we fill out this application, something good will come of it, okay?"

I threw up my hands, surrendering.

And so we made an account and began to fill in the application. I couldn't believe how long the thing was—page after page after page of inane questions: *What are your life goals? How do you think Columbia could help you reach these goals? Is there anything in your record that you think bears explanation (if so, please provide that explanation in the box below)? What was the single most important experience of your life?*

"Start writing, buddy."

I scrawled an answer to the first question as quickly as I could, then tore the page out of my notebook and handed it to Zelda. She typed it into the application site, making changes and corrections as she went, while I set to work on the next question. We fell into a sort of rhythm, and within a couple of hours, we'd finished the whole thing. Or the part we *could* finish, at any rate.

"It says here that you need recommendations," Zelda said. "Who would do that for you?"

No one.

"I refuse to believe that. What about a teacher?"

I don't even remember my teachers.

"But I bet your teachers remember you. You're very memorable."

Suddenly Danny Wu's head appeared over our computer monitor. "Mr. McArthur would do it," he said.

Sometime in the past few minutes, the Call of Duty game had ended, and now three of my fellow Chess & War students were standing above our computer, staring at Zelda like she was some kind of space alien. Danny was co-captain of the school's chess team. With him were Maya Leung and Tom Wilson, another couple of standard-issue dorks.

"Who's Mr. McArthur?" Zelda asked, but just then Danny was distracted by my black eye.

"That's a real shiner you've got there, Parker! Did Tyler do that to you? Alana told me that something went down at a movie theater or something, but I thought she was full of it."

I began to write a response, but Danny interrupted me.

"I understand sign language, if you wanna do that instead." He finished the thought in sign: *My little brother's deaf, so I had to learn.*

Why didn't you ever tell me? I signed back.

I don't know. We don't ever talk.

"Did you know the first significant deaf community in America was started on Martha's Vineyard?" Maya said, interrupting our silent conversation. "I did a whole report on it. They even had their own form of sign language."

"So who's your friend, Parker?" Tom asked.

Zelda put out a hand. "I'm Zelda."

"Really? What an epic name! Have you played any of the Zelda games, like on Nintendo?"

"Sadly, no."

"Bummer. They're so freaking good. Like there's this one where you have to save the world before this planet crashes into Hyrule, and you have to keep living the same three days over and over again, and it's super tense—"

"Tom?" Danny said.

"Yeah."

"Maybe save the video-game synopsis for lunch?"

Tom grinned. He was famous for his ability to jabber on endlessly about anything, and also impossible to shame. "Deal. You'll get the whole franchise history."

"Nice to meet you, Zelda," Danny said. "I'm Danny, and this is Tom and Maya." Everybody shook hands. "So what are you guys doing in here?"

"I'm helping Parker with his college applications," Zelda said.

"Really?" Maya said. "Where are you applying?" She craned her neck around until she could see our screen. "Columbia? That's Ivy League! Do you really think you can get in there?"

I shook my head emphatically.

"Don't be so sure," Danny said. "I mean, you *are* a minority. And a good one too. Like, I'm Chinese, which is basically useless. Nobody in Stanford admissions is sitting around thinking, 'I wish we could finally find some academically successful Chinese kids,' you know?"

"I hear that," Maya said.

"Hey, you don't know struggle until you've tried being a white man in this country," Tom said. "Even if I get a job, I'm only going to make, like, thirty percent more than a woman. Just twenty years ago, I would've made double."

Maya rolled her eyes. "Hilarious, Tom."

"Danny," Zelda said, "you mentioned a teacher who might write a recommendation?"

"Yeah. Mr. McArthur. He taught our ninth-grade English class."

"Do you remember him, Parker?"

Of course I remembered him. He was pretty much the only teacher I'd ever had that I actually liked, the only one who'd assigned the class science-fiction and fantasy books to read (most teachers treat that kind of stuff as if it's all crap, because they're too stupid to question what *they* learned as kids). It was Mr. McArthur who got me started inventing stuff, instead of just journaling, with this vocabulary exercise where we had to write stories using one new word in every sentence.

That was three years ago, I signed.

"So what?" Danny said. "I still remember the stories you

wrote. Zelda, Parker wrote the *best* stories. Most of us just ended up with gibberish, because we had to use words like 'Brobdingnagian' in every sentence."

"Brobdingnagian," Tom recited, "meaning 'gigantic,' from Jonathan Swift's *Gulliver's Travels*. Now where's my gold star?"

"But Parker," Danny went on, "he actually wrote real stories. There was this one about a spaceship that got lost and ended up orbiting the moon until everyone on it was dead. Mr. McArthur read it aloud for the whole class."

"So you think he'd write Parker a recommendation?" Zelda said.

"Definitely."

She clapped with excitement. "Perfect! Let's call him now."

Wait, I signed.

But Tom was already on his way out of the room. "I'll get a directory," he called over his shoulder.

We don't need to do this right now, I wrote.

"No time like the present, darling," Zelda said. Tom came back in with the directory and found Mr. McArthur's name. Zelda made the call.

"Hello, is this"—she checked the directory—"Edward McArthur? Oh good. My name is Zelda Toth, and I'm the application adviser for a student named Parker Santé. Is this name familiar to you?" She smiled at me. "Oh, it is! Wonderful! So I was hoping you might be willing to write a recommendation for Parker. He can't ask himself because . . .

exactly. Really? You, sir, are a hero! Thank you so much. I have your e-mail address right here, actually. I'll send you the form in a few minutes. Yes. Yes, thank you. All right. Goodbye." She hung up the phone. "Ta-da!"

As Danny and the rest of the chess crew applauded, Zelda suddenly gave me a 6.8-on-the-passion-scale kiss. Tom hooted, while Danny and Maya carried out a brief dialogue of raised eyebrows. In the last five minutes, I'd gone from a nobody slacker with a speech disorder to a secret Casanova with a mega-hot girlfriend and hopes of attending an Ivy League university.

"So we were all going to get some lunch over at the Embarcadero," Tom said, once the applause died down. "You guys should come with."

"Sure," Zelda said, speaking for both of us. "Just give us an hour. I think we should get started on at least one other application, don't you, Parker?"

I nodded, but it was a few seconds before I realized I wasn't pretending anymore. Mr. McArthur had agreed to write my recommendation, and none of the chess kids had treated me like I was crazy to be trying for a good school. So why not go for it?

Just no Ivy League this time, okay? Somebody here has to be realistic.

"Really?" Zelda said. "But why?"

LUNCH OF THE NERDS

APPARENTLY, THIS WHOLE UNDERTAKING— a few hours of Call of Duty followed by lunch down by the water—was a weekly occurrence for the Chess & War kids, and had been since the beginning of the year. But I was still surprised to see Alana waiting for us when we got to Mad Pizza. She sat before a congealed slice of pepperoni and a pile of soggy pool-noodle fries, acknowledging us with a barely perceptible head nod. With everything that had happened between me and Zelda in the past twenty-four hours, I'd almost forgotten that Alana and her boyfriend had broken up yesterday, and in spectacular fashion.

Zelda and I sat down across from her while the others went to order.

"What are you doing here?" Zelda asked.

"I come every week," Alana said in a self-consciously tragic monotone. "I thought it would cheer me up."

"And?"

She shook her head. "My food tastes like shit."

I picked up one of her fries and crammed it into my mouth. *Tastes fine to me,* I wrote in my notebook, then spun it around so she could read.

"It's a manifestation of my sadness, dumbass. Fries stop tasting good."

"Obviously," Zelda said.

"I think it's one of the classic stages of grief. Like stage two, maybe. Or whichever one comes right after the stage where you delete every Facebook photo of you and your ex and right before the stage where you sneak into his house in the middle of the night and set his dick on fire." She closed her eyes, took a deep breath, then opened them again. "Nice Moleskine, by the way."

"I bought it for him," Zelda said.

"Of course you did." She pointed an accusatory fry at Zelda, punctuating each word with a little fry-thrust. "Because you . . . don't . . . suck . . . ass." She squeezed the fry in her fist until its potatoey innards ran out between her knuckles. "You know what Tyler always bought me? Flowers. I fucking hate flowers. What kind of asshole buys you something that you have to take care of? 'Here you go, person I supposedly love, here's an additional responsibility for you. And if you fail in your duties, you'll have a flowery corpse on your hands. You're welcome!' That's the opposite of a present. That's a fucking *un*present!"

She was panting now, her face red and her hand covered in fry guts. "All I'm trying to say is hold on to this one, Parker. She's the real thing."

Yeah, I wrote in my journal, *you'd never just disappear on me, would you, Zelda?*

"How can you even ask her that?" Alana said. "Of course she wouldn't."

Zelda gave me a meaningful look, but she didn't say anything.

The rest of the Chess & War kids returned to the table. Danny, Maya, and Tom were now joined by Gabrielle Okimoto, Narun Vasher, and Steven Wong. I didn't know any of them particularly well (aside from the fact that I was better at chess than Narun and Steven, and significantly worse than Gabrielle), but none of them seemed surprised that I'd shown up for the pizza party.

"So how did you two meet?" Tom asked. "I'm always amazed when anyone from our walk of life acquires a lover."

"He tried to rob me at the Palace Hotel," Zelda said. "Then I told him I was immortal. We've been inseparable ever since."

There was silence for a moment, and then Steven piped up. He was a small kid with thick hipster glasses, famous for scoring a perfect 2400 on his SAT.

"Like the hydra," he said.

Zelda scrunched up her forehead. "The what?"

"The hydra. It's kinda like a jellyfish. Never ages, as far as anyone can tell, and if you cut it into pieces, the pieces grow into whole new hydras. And there's another one that can do this rad Benjamin Button thing where it grows into an adult, then turns back into a polyp and grows up all over again."

"Sea urchins don't age either," Maya said. "Or lobsters, I think. Or clams."

Tom made a face. "I hate clams. They taste like ocean-flavored snot."

"Gross."

"You could also argue that bacteria are immortal," Danny

226

said. "They divide into perfect copies of themselves indefinitely. But as for people . . . it's a no go."

"I believe that is only a matter of time," Narun said. He was maybe the most humorless person in Chess & War, and he got really angry whenever he lost a game. "My father says that soon we will all upload our brains into the cloud."

"What will our brains do in the clouds?" Zelda asked.

Everyone laughed, thinking she was joking. *The cloud means computers,* I wrote. *Like the Internet and stuff.*

"Actually, I don't even know *why* people age," Maya said. "I mean, it seems pretty stupid, from an evolutionary perspective."

"Nobody knows for sure," Danny said.

Really? I signed. *No one?*

"There are theories."

"I've heard them all," Zelda said, "as you would expect, given that I'm immortal." Another laugh, though this time it was everybody else who didn't get the joke. "A biologist named Peter Medawar believed that nature was so brutal, there'd be no reason for animals to have the genes for immortality, because they'd inevitably be eaten anyway. But that makes no sense, because aging *causes* a lot of animals to be eaten."

"My grandmother's slow as shit," Tom said. "Why hasn't anyone eaten her?"

"Shut up, Tom," Maya said. "Zelda, please continue."

"After Medawar, the prevailing theory was that there must be some advantage granted by genes that make us age, and we simply haven't figured out what it is. But we've found a lot of genes associated with aging, and many don't have any corresponding benefit. Another theory is that the body is meant to be disposable, just a means of transmitting genetic material between generations, so it purposely devotes most of its resources to making babies, instead of taking care of itself."

"That makes sense," Narun said.

"In theory. But studies show that when people eat less, they end up living longer, which means excess resources still don't increase longevity."

Tom paused with his pizza slice halfway to his mouth. "So if I eat this, I'm gonna die sooner?"

"Maybe."

"Fuck it." He took a bite, then talked with his mouth full. "Live fast, die young, eat pepperoni. That's my motto."

So what's the answer? I wrote.

"Danny is right," Zelda said. "No one knows. Aging flies in the face of everything we know about evolution, but all the research points to the idea that it serves a purpose."

"God," Gabrielle said.

There was a collective groan from the assembly of scientists-in-training.

"What?" Gabrielle said defensively. "God and science are not incompatible. And Zelda just said it herself. Nothing adds up unless you consider God."

"Which God?" Narun said.

"Oh, don't get all political on me. It doesn't matter. Kali. Buddha. Freaking Cthulhu if that's your jam. I'm just saying we all know the real reason why people get old and die. Because if life went on forever and ever, it would suck. And only some sort of god could reason that out."

I could already see the direction the conversation was going: this was exactly what I *didn't* want Zelda to have to think about.

Can we change the subject? I signed to Danny, but he wasn't paying attention.

"Why do you say that living forever would suck?" Zelda asked.

"I don't know," Gabrielle said. "It's just—I spend most of my life thinking about the future, right? It's the whole reason I do everything I do. But if I knew the future was going to go on forever, suddenly there'd be no reason to try. Why would I even bother getting out of bed in the morning?"

"Yeah," Danny said. "And just think of your friends and your family. You'd have to go to about a million funerals."

"It's like when someone buys you flowers," Alana said. "You're expected to stand around and watch them die. If you lived forever, you'd have to do that with people. It would be, like, a nonstop death parade."

Everyone at the table was quiet for a moment, recognizing that the discussion had taken a pretty dark turn. I think Narun was trying to lighten the mood when he turned things back to Zelda. "So is it true?"

"Is what true?" she asked.

"Well, you're the immortal here. Is that what it's like? A nonstop death parade?"

Zelda took her time answering, long enough that I could sense everyone starting to get a little nervous. It wasn't as if they actually believed she was immortal, but we were really just talking about death, and no one could be sure how much Zelda knew about *that* subject. Whether you're twelve or eighty or two hundred, no one can ever tell what you've been through just by looking at you. Only boxers and junkies wear their scars where people can see them.

"Parker and I went to see a Seurat exhibit yesterday," she finally said. "You know him?"

"The dots guy," Steven said.

"Exactly. The dots guy. I've always thought getting older was a bit like looking at those paintings. You're born, and that's when you're standing right up next to the canvas. Nothing makes any sense. There's just a lot of light and color. But as you get older, you begin to back away, and that's when the image starts to cohere. All those little spots of color turn into flowers, or people, or dogs. You gain perspective. But when you live forever . . . that is, *if* you were to live forever, you would have to keep backing away, and pretty soon the painting would just be a square of brightness way off in the distance. You could still remember what it looked like when you were closer, but you wouldn't really be seeing it anymore. And then you'd keep moving away from it, until you couldn't even make out color anymore, until the painting was just this single point of light. And then it would be swallowed up in the darkness around it, like a star winking out. The grief would be so huge, don't you think? Not just because you'd lose the people you love—we all have to do that—but because you'd have so much perspective. You'd see the terrible sweep of history, repeating its tragedies over and over again. You'd sink under all that time like a scuttled ship."

After Zelda finished speaking, the only sound in the restaurant was the cheesy Italian music piped through the speakers.

"Fuck me," Tom eventually said. "I think I'd just kill myself."

I stood up from the table. *We should go,* I signed.

"Already?" Danny said. "We were going to go back to the computer lab for some more Call of Duty."

Zelda and I have somewhere to be.

I didn't bother saying more than that, just took hold of Zelda's hand and helped her out of her seat.

"It was a pleasure meeting all of you," she said. "Have wonderful lives."

"You too," Danny said, confused.

Outside, a light rain was falling, and the sky looked like an enormous gray balloon that would drench the whole city if you could get at it with a pin. Zelda's eyes were far away, just like they'd been when I'd first seen her in the Palace Hotel, as still and sorrowful as an old statue in an empty square.

S-o-r-r-y, I finger spelled.

"Why? It's just the truth."

I shook my head.

"It is, though."

I shook my head again, more emphatically this time, and I hated that shaking my head was all I had. Why couldn't I scream "No!" at the top of my lungs, like a normal person?

"Yes it is, Parker! I know it and you know it and even your friends know it."

I opened up my journal again and filled up a whole page with that one word—*No*—but it was just a word on a piece of paper, silent as a gravestone. I turned to the next page. *I'm still going to prove to you that life is worth living. Just tell me what you want. I'll do anything.*

Zelda made a little scream of exasperation. "What about you? What do you want, Parker?"

I want to make you happy.

For some reason, this answer made Zelda even angrier. She knocked the journal out of my hands. One of my expensive new pens clattered onto the pavement and rolled into a storm drain.

"You say you want to convince me that life is worth living? Then you'll have to tell me what it is that makes you want to live. Because as far as I can see, it's nothing." She spat this last word out. "All these young people I've met in the past couple of days, the ones who ought to be your friends—they're meeting you the same way they're meeting me. But they've known you for years. So where have you been, Parker? How have you managed to hide out right in the middle of your own life?"

I could only shrug.

"There it is again. You shrug." She shoved me. "Who knows?" She shoved me again. "Who cares?" She shoved me again, so that I stumbled off the curb and ended up in the middle of the road. "Why don't you stay right there? Pretty soon a car'll come along and finish the job for you." I took a step in Zelda's direction, and she put out her hands to block me. "No! Don't you come back here unless you're ready to be a person. A real person, I mean— the kind who feels things and tries things and *wants* things. Can you do that? Because if you can't, then you should just throw in the towel right now. Both of us should."

I knew she was right. For such a long time, I hadn't let myself want anything, or nothing important anyway. It felt safer that way. But the truth is I *did* want things now: I wanted to go to college, and I wanted to speak, and I wanted Zelda to stay with me. And maybe more than anything, I wanted to tell her that I wanted her. And I couldn't hide behind not having words, because I didn't need words for this.

I reached out and pulled her down into the roadway with me. I looked into those ocean eyes, and pushed her silver hair back over her ears. And then I kissed her, a kiss that went on and on until she couldn't misinterpret what it was I wanted. And when she finally pulled away, she didn't laugh or smile. It freaked me out, actually, how utterly serious she looked.

"So take me home, Parker."

SAUDADE

DON'T EVEN GET ME STARTED ON THE fucking birds and the bees. Like, why would we teach kids about sex that way? I assume you already know this, but it still blows my mind that when people talk about that shit, they're not actually talking about birds having flappy beaky sex with other birds, or bees having buzzy stingy sex with other bees. They're talking about how birds and bees help *flowers* have sex by unintentionally picking up pollen on their bodies when they're flying around collecting nectar. As far as I know, that is not how people do it.

My mom on sex: "Try to do it mostly with people you love. Use protection. Don't be an asshole."

My dad on sex (from an article he wrote in some magazine): "Having sex is twenty times easier than writing about it."

D'Angelo on sex: "My darling/You aren't the average kind/You need the comfort of my lovin'/To bring out the best in you."

So what to do? Writing about what happened between me and Zelda seems like the very definition of TMI. But wouldn't passing over it completely be a pretty serious (dare I say it?) anticlimax? I mean, people *say* they like stories where boy meets girl and then boy gets girl. But I think people don't care so much about the "get" part as long as there's a "gets it on with" part. And I promised at the beginning of this whole saga that I wasn't going to pretend sex didn't exist just because I'm who I am and you're who you are. So let's just take it nice and slow. Don't be nervous. I know you aren't the average kind.

When we got back to the house, I saw my mom's car in the driveway, which was bad news. I'd either have to totally ignore her, or else hash out the fight all over again. But I got lucky (pun entirely intended): the house was empty. I didn't know where my mom was, and honestly, I didn't care. Zelda and I went straight up to my room and sat down on the bed, and I thought about how less than two days ago we'd been right here and she'd said, "I'm not going to have sex with you tonight," and there was a part of me that wished she'd say it again, because the moment of truth was coming and I was terrified of it. But she didn't. I started to take off my shirt, but Zelda stopped me.

"Let me do that. It's always better to be undressed than to undress yourself."

I didn't know what to do with my hands or my face, so I just sat there, still as a mannequin, while she unbuttoned the shirt she'd bought for me. It flashed through my head that this girl was actually older than my great-great-great-great-great-great-great grandmother would've been. And was it weird that I wasn't more weirded out by that fact?

"Hey," Zelda said. "Get out of your head. I'm right here."

Yes, she was. We finished undressing each other and got into bed. The house was just cold enough that it felt really good under the covers, skin to skin. And then we were kissing, and then it was happening, and I'll just leave the gory details to your imagination, if that's okay by you.

Afterward, Zelda lay next to me with her eyes closed. "I've missed this," she said. "And I didn't even know it. Fancy that." She slid her head up into the curve of my neck. I remember thinking how amazing it was, all the million ways that human bodies fit together. "Nathaniel and I stopped sleeping together when he turned fifty. It was his decision. He said it felt wrong to be like that with me. For a while after that, he treated me like a daughter. Then, as his health began to fail, I started treating him like a son. It's all very strange." I laughed. That was the understatement of the fucking century. "Anyway, it's all in the past now. There's no need to discuss it. Really, we should be napping. You haven't learned this yet, but the afterglow is the absolute best time for napping."

I lay there watching her, as her breath deepened and her face relaxed. There's a word in Portuguese that my dad wrote about in one of his books: *saudade*. It's the sadness you feel for something that isn't gone yet, but will be. The sadness of lost causes. The sadness of being alive.

I intertwined my legs with Zelda's legs, my arms with her arms, as if I could hold on to her just by holding on to her. We fell asleep wrapped up in each other like a couple of tangled cables, the kind that are so knotted up in so many places that the only way you could separate them would be with a pair of scissors. And that would ruin one of them for good. Maybe even both of them.

I woke up an hour later, with the sun framed perfectly in the window, a yellow corona of light suspended in the white fog like an egg yolk.

I grabbed my journal off the side table and sat up in bed.

Zelda mumbled some gibberish in her sleep, or maybe something in a foreign tongue. I started to write.

STORY #3:
BRAVERY

AFTER THE BATTLE OF CROSSED EYES, THE
greatest warriors of the tribe were brought before King Uthor
to receive prizes for their valor. First came Christos, also called
the Limb Collector, because he kept a collection of his enemies'
severed arms and legs in a pile outside his hut. His prize was a
fine ax of wrought gold. Next came Boris, also called Ironskin,
who was seven feet tall and the same around, who wore no
armor because his body was his armor, who had been wounded
so many times that any new injury he sustained was likely just
the opening of an old scar. His gift was a fine black stallion, as
he'd broken the back of his previous mount when attempting to
leap onto it during the battle. Finally the greatest warrior of the
tribe was brought forward. His name was Klaus, though most
everyone called him the Dragon's Head because, like the fear-
some fire-breathing head of a dragon, he led every charge.

King Uthor was effusive in his praise, as everyone in the
tribe knew that the day would've been lost if not for Klaus. The
queen could only blush when the great warrior knelt at her feet
and kissed her hand (in truth, she had always carried a flame
for Klaus, who risked his brawny, beautiful body day after day,

while her husband, though a good king, had grown soft and flabby over the years). For his bravery, Klaus was granted an enormous bronze bathing tub, built to be heated over a flame like a cooking pot, along with the usual spoils of a war well-waged: gold and gems, slaves and such.

Now it came to pass that around this time, a mystic was said to be wandering the outskirts of the tribe's territories. Reports of her physical aspect varied. Some said she was a wizened crone, hunched over like the top of a shepherd's crook, leading an equally wizened donkey behind her. Others said she was a young woman of uncommon beauty, raven-haired but for a single streak of silver that fell across her forehead like a lightning bolt, and riding a fine white horse. It was in this latter guise that she was discovered a few days later by two of the tribe's scouts. She had just been attacked by bandits, and surely would've been killed had the scouts not come to her aid.

In gratitude, she told them to send a message to their king. She would make camp in the glade of her salvation for three days. During that time, she would provide a free reading for one person each night, at precisely midnight. But her message didn't end there. She told the scouts to warn their king that a reading was a gift, but it could also be a curse.

"The truth," she said, "is not for the pusillanimous."

When King Uthor received this message, he was overjoyed. Lately he'd worried that his time as king had rendered him feeble and fainthearted. He couldn't help but notice that his wife, the queen, didn't seem as excited by him as she'd once been. In the beginning, just after he'd first won her hand for his brave acts during the Battle of Ardor's Fall, she'd been an insatiable lover. Now her only insatiable desires were for plums and sleep.

And so, the very next night, he set off for the glade in which the mystic had made camp. There was a strange silence in the forest, and the king was reminded of his younger days, back when he was just a warrior himself, before he'd been elected king by the tribe's council of elders. He remembered how he would be sick with fear before every great battle, certain he would not return. That dread returned to him now, as he moved through the dark and forbidding forest. Every owl's hoot and twig's crack was a presentiment of his own death. He was shaking with terror by the time he caught sight of a torch flickering between the branches of the trees. The mystic sat cross-legged before a smooth stump on which various painted cards were laid out. She was neither an old crone nor a beautiful young woman. In fact, she appeared exactly as Uthor's mother had, back when the king was just a little boy inventing great battles for himself, playing alone in the forest. He went to her and fell weeping into her arms.

"Quiet," the mystic said softly, stroking the back of his head.

"But I am weak, Mother," the king said. "I no longer go out to war with the rest of my tribe. I stay safe in my tent while I send others to die."

"When you were a warrior, you feared death, yet still you fought. As a king, you fear being called a coward, yet you do your duty and remain safe in your tent for the sake of your tribe. Be at peace, my son, for I have read your soul in the cards. You are a brave man."

And though the words were simple, the king felt them land with the certainty of arrows in his heart. When he returned to his palatial hut, he couldn't help but rouse his beautiful queen. Even in the wan light, she could see the joy in his face.

"You must speak with the mystic," the king said. "She has made a new man of me." And then he took the queen in his arms and kissed her with the passion of youth.

The following night, the queen put on her many furs and ventured out into the woods. It had been a long time since she had been allowed to travel alone. Only as a young girl, before she'd been betrothed to the king, had she had such liberty. Unlike her husband, the queen had no fear of the darkness. In fact, she felt herself growing lighter with each step she took. She let fall her furs so the cool air could wrap itself around her bare limbs. She shimmied up trees so she could see how the moonlight glittered on the canopy of the forest. From one of these perches, she sighted the mystic's encampment, and she approached it like a child told to go to bed, sneaking back downstairs to listen to the grown-ups speak of grown-up things.

At first she was confused, because there was no woman in the glade at all. Instead a man sat on the tree stump, smoking a long pipe and watching the stars. It was her father, who'd brokered her marriage to the king many years ago. He'd been dead many a year now. She ran to him, leaped up on his lap, and buried her head in his shoulder.

"Quiet," the mystic said softly, stroking the back of the queen's head.

"But I am weak, Father," the queen said. "I fantasize of a man who isn't my husband, that we will run away together and leave everything and everyone behind."

"When you were a girl, your greatest joy was dancing alone in the woods, yet you allowed yourself to be married when duty demanded it. As queen, you dream of escape, yet you accept the confining yoke of leadership. Be at peace, my daughter, for I have read your soul in the cards. You are a brave woman."

The queen did not skip back through the forest, though she knew she could have if she'd wanted to. Instead she walked slowly, savoring these last few moments alone. The sun was coming up, and she slipped into bed just as the king was waking. He always rose early, to ride the length and breadth of the tribe's territory and ask after the welfare of his subjects. She had never loved him more than she did at that moment.

"Did you meet the mystic?" he asked.

"Yes. It was wonderful."

"Good." He kissed her forehead. "We have one more reading to bestow. Who do you think should receive it?"

The king and the queen decided that Klaus the Dragon's Head, who had done so much for their tribe over the years, deserved the honor.

When Klaus received the news, he was disappointed. He had no interest in speaking with some madwoman in the woods—not when he could be back in his hut, soaking in his steaming bronze tub of lavender-scented water with a few slave girls. Also, this gift that the king and queen deemed "priceless" might cost him other, more conventionally valuable gifts (that golden ax Christos had received would've made for a much better prize). Still, Klaus knew he could not refuse the offer, so when night fell, he begrudgingly entered the forest. He did not notice the stars or the moon. He didn't skip or climb trees, nor did he tremble with fear at the hoot of an owl. He arrived in the mystic's glade in half the time it had taken either the king or the queen. There, his last hope—that he would meet the beautiful woman with the white streak in her raven-black hair—was dashed. It was a little girl waiting for him in front of the tree stump. Her hair was silver, her eyes the color of the ocean, and her expression was imperious and patronizing.

"Child, where is the mystic?" Klaus asked.

"I have read your soul in the cards," the girl said. "Are you prepared to hear your judgment?"

"I suppose," Klaus said, picking an errant piece of goat meat out from between his two front teeth.

"You must be certain. Because it is more likely that you are prepared to hear what you have always heard. That you are the bravest among men. That your strength is beyond measure. That you are quick and clever and gallant. But this is idle flattery. This is small minds chattering to themselves. I offer you the truth."

Klaus noticed an unfamiliar gnawing at the bottom of his stomach. He wouldn't even have been able to give it a name, so novel was the feeling. But the queen would've recognized it. She had felt it the moment that her father told her she'd been promised to Uthor. And the king would have recognized it too. He'd felt it every day he went out into battle as a young warrior.

"Out with it," Klaus said, only why was his throat so very dry?

"Very well," the girl said. "You are a coward."

"Me? A coward?" Klaus laughed his usual laugh, the one that echoed like a thunderclap as he charged toward his enemies. In the glade of the mystic, it sounded thin and false.

"Yes."

"You are new to this region, little girl, so perhaps you haven't yet heard tales of my triumphs. At the Battle of Crossed Eyes, I was disarmed early in the day, and I went on to kill twenty men with my bare hands. At the Battle of Blood Creek, I was responsible for the blood creek in question. At the Battle of Death Hill, I was shot full of so many arrows that some of my own tribesmen mistook me for a gigantic porcupine. I am the first to lead any charge, and the last to leave the battlefield. I am Klaus, the Dragon's Head."

"And I say again you are a coward, Klaus the Dragon's Buttock!"

244

This short sentence struck Klaus like a fist to the gut, and he fell down onto his knees.

"You lead the charge because you wish to be known as the man who leads the charge," the girl said. "You have never feared the dark, and you have never feared pain, and you have never feared the enemy. And where there is no fear, there is no bravery."

As the girl continued to speak, Klaus imagined himself shrinking, word by word, inch by inch, until he felt certain he'd become a tiny child, younger even than the mystic.

"There is only one thing that truly frightens you, Klaus the Dragon's Testicles."

"What is it?" he asked, truly desperate to know.

"The moment when the last bard singing of your exploits holds his hand to his heart and keels over. When the last man who heard those songs is laid to rest in the ground. You fear oblivion, Klaus the Dragon's Arse. And every time you run headlong into battle, you are running from that fear."

"Tell me what to do," Klaus said. "Teach me to be brave."

"I cannot." And for the first time, there was at least a spark of sympathy in the mystic's eyes. "Your reading is done. My debt to your people is repaid."

For a moment, a bank of clouds covered up the moon and the stars, cloaking the glade in darkness. When the light returned, the mystic had disappeared. The only sign that she'd ever existed was a single white card left on the stump. It showed a smiling man in motley holding a dragon's-head staff: *The Fool.*

Klaus did not return to his tribe that night, or ever again. People said that the mystic must have fallen in love with him, and they'd run away together. Other, less romantic folk said that he'd been beset by a large group of highwaymen on the way home and killed. Months passed. The stories of Klaus the Dragon's Head grew into legends, told to the youngest warriors of the tribe, to inspire them before battle. Years passed. While the legends of Klaus were no longer told in the tents of war (having been replaced by the valorous history of Kong the Destroyer), they were still recited by parents to their sleepless children, as bedtime stories. In these stories, Klaus fought against magical creatures—wizards and faeries and elves—and defeated them not only with brute strength, but with cunning. Decades passed. The tribe was massacred by another, larger tribe. And that very night, the warriors of the conquering tribe began to tell stories of Bandino the Blade, who'd led them to victory by killing a hundred men with a dagger no longer than his pinky. The bodies of all the tribesmen who'd ever heard the stories of Klaus the Dragon's Head were buried in a long trench. Their heads, mute now, were mounted on pikes around the village.

ARRESTED

OKAY, I'LL ADMIT THAT I DIDN'T WRITE EVERY word of that at the time, but I did get the broad strokes of the story down. (And you can't expect me not to give these things a bit of a polish before showing them to you. Remember: I'm dumb, not stupid.)

"Can I read it?" Zelda asked. I hadn't even noticed she'd woken up.

I passed her the journal. While she read, I let my gaze float around the room. It felt different in here now, after what had happened between us. My eyes came to rest on the photograph mounted on the wall right in front of the bed. It had been taken at San Diego Comic-Con, just a month or so before my dad died. The organizers of the convention had given him a table in a lonely corner of the "Autograph Arena," and he and I spent the whole afternoon sitting there, waiting for people to ask him to sign their books. I can still remember the desperation of that place—the desperation of second-tier actors, of comic-book guys who actually looked like the Comic-Book Guy from *The Simpsons*, of fan clubs and fanzines and blogs about blogs and blogs. The desperation of indoor kids seeking their first nondigital friendships—maybe even a furtive hookup in the back row of a screening of the trailer for the next Batman movie. Near my dad's table, some actor sat behind a little doppelgänger army of cardboard cutouts of himself dressed as a hobbit; apparently, he'd had a role in one of the Lord of the Rings movies. The line stretching away from his table was long—like waiting-for-a-lifeboat-on-the-deck-of-the-Titanic long—while the line in front of my dad's table was not. In fact, it didn't even deserve the geometric designation "line." Occasionally, it was a dot. Usually it was nothing. Void. The total absence of attention. This photograph was taken during one of the dot periods. Just me, my dad, and some pimply teenage advertisement for celibacy who'd loved my dad's first book.

I saw that photo the moment I woke up every morning, and it was usually the last thing I saw before I went to bed. And why? Just to prove to myself that I hadn't forgotten him?

"That's a good one," Zelda said, handing me back the notebook. "But I have to ask—what inspired it? I haven't known many men who write short stories postcoitally."

It's for my applications. I want you to see I'm serious about going to college.

"I know you are, darling."

She kissed me on the cheek.

But do you really think I'm arrested? I wrote.

"I think you're arrest*ing*," she said with a smile.

I'm being serious. Yesterday you told my mom you thought I was arrested. Did you mean it?

She wrapped her arms around me. "Yes. But I didn't say it to be hurtful. And I think things are already changing. Can't you feel it?"

I nodded. The rain was playing music on the shingles over our head. Out the attic window I saw it patter on the crooked trees and bent weathervanes and wrought-iron fences of the Sunset. I've always liked the rain, maybe because I grew up with it always coming around. It kept things clean. It washed things away. I'd often wondered what people did in cities where it never rained. How could they ever start fresh?

"Where are you going?" Zelda asked.

I climbed out of bed and down the attic ladder. In the kitchen, I got a garbage bag out from under the sink. The only question was where to begin.

SYMBOLIC GESTURES

I NOTICED THE ONE ABOVE THE TELEVISION first, because how could I miss it? How could anyone miss a foot-tall photograph in a wide silver frame, its subject staring down at you like some sort of judgmental religious icon every time you just wanted to relax with the tube? When I took it down, a rectangular shadow of white was left on the wall. It reminded me of this photograph we'd seen in history class, taken in Hiroshima after the bomb had been dropped, in which someone's silhouette had been permanently etched into the cement by the force of the blast.

In the kitchen, a tiny photograph of the three of us at Disneyland hung from a nail above the toaster. I'd had it framed for my mom last Christmas. In the picture, I was small and chubby, smiling hugely, with a pair of black plastic mouse ears on my head. My mom wore a neon fanny pack. There was a crack of splintering glass when it landed in the garbage bag with the other photo.

Three different pictures were mounted on the wall of the stairway. One of them was a cartoon someone had drawn, in which my dad's stubbly beard became a wide bush with a bird inside it and my mom's tiny ears had been transformed into mere nubs on the side of her head. *NYC, 2004* was written at the bottom. *Crack.* Next to that was a wedding photograph, taken at some epically shitty photography studio. My parents were posed against a swirly blue background, spooning standing, the way people always stood in pictures but never stood in real life. My mom's dress made her look like a cheap cupcake, and my dad's suit made him look like a bad waiter. *Crack.* The topmost picture was again of all three of us, but I was just a baby in this one. My parents were co-cradling me, staring down at me with this look in their eyes like this kid was going to be the solution to all their problems. *Crack.*

The upstairs hallway was a veritable museum of photographs, and it included the true centerpiece of the collection. At first glance, the image in question looked pretty ordinary—hardly deserving of the big bronze frame. My dad was sitting on the couch in front of his laptop, looking up at the camera with his usual annoyance.

It was the last photograph we had of him, taken just a week before the accident. *Crack.*

In my mom's room, I did my best not to look at the photos as I picked them up and dropped them into the bag, but I accidentally caught sight of one that had been taken on our trip to Colombia, in which my dad and I were making a sand castle on the beach. The whole trip came rushing back to me in one enormous wave-crash of memories. My dad had rented a metal detector, so we could search up and down the beach for hidden treasures. All we ever found were a bunch of bottle caps and some loose change, but those were treasures enough for a five-year-old. I could remember my dad speaking Spanish with the hotel staff and the owners of local shops and the men who walked up and down the beach selling costume jewelry and bottled water. He seemed so at home there, so much happier than he ever was in California. *Crack.*

I left the bag at the bottom of the ladder and climbed back up into my bedroom. There was only the one photograph here. I pulled it off the wall and dropped it down to the second floor. *Crash.*

Zelda sat up in bed, alarmed. "Parker, what are you doing?"

I-t-s f-i-n-e, I finger spelled.

And of course I knew this was all just symbolic. Somewhere in my mom's room, there was a whole cardboard box full of other photos. But I wasn't trying to eradicate every trace of my father. I was trying to make a point. To my mom, and to myself, and maybe most importantly, to Zelda. Because if I could move on, then maybe she could too. Maybe we could move on together.

I picked up her clothes and brought them to her in bed.

"Are you okay?" she asked.

I nodded, then gestured that she should get dressed. I was about to head back downstairs when I remembered the box under the bed. Zelda helped me get it down the ladder, and then we dumped it out into the garbage bag.

Outside, the rain was pelting down, and I ran for the trash can.

"That's the first place your mom will look, you know," Zelda said.

Damn. I hadn't thought of that. Why did big symbolic gestures have to be so complicated? I put the bag down in the driveway and went back inside to get the keys.

"Where are we going?" Zelda asked, once we were in the car.

I shrugged, because I didn't know yet. I just started driving, up Oak Street and across the Panhandle, the rain growing more intense every second, through Hayes Valley and then spiraling up onto the Central Freeway, heading south but exiting on Cesar Chavez when I finally figured out what I had to do, then getting back on the freeway heading in the other direction. Every few hundred feet, a long black scrape ran along the cement wall of the highway. Each one represented some kind of accident. Most of them had probably been small. Others had probably been just like mine—a gaping hole opening up in the fabric of reality, a sadness that no one else could see pouring in like water through a leak in a boat. I stopped just shy of the yellow-black stripes of the divider separating the 80 and the 101. Ground zero.

I set the bag on the hood of the car and then climbed up next to it. Cars streaked by in glow-stick lines, flashing white to red as they passed. The hood was slippery with rain. I stepped to the edge of it and, with a grunt, emptied the bag over the triangular divider, into the no-man's-land just beyond the apex. The glass in the frames shattered on the pavement, and the papers rose upward, carried by the wind from the passing cars in fractal fluttering patterns, like enormous flakes of ash, plastering themselves to windshields, pulled under the tires of big rigs, disappearing over the walls of the highway and gone forever.

I noticed one of my dad's diaries had landed just on top of the cement divider. Zelda reached out with her foot and kicked it off. She looked at me and smiled. "We ought to get out of here. Otherwise, I think we're going to be arrested for felony littering."

YOUR TURN

I BACKED UP A FEW FEET AND TOOK THE off-ramp. I felt electrified, both from being so close to all those rushing cars, and from letting go of all that *past* at once. But my excitement was quickly overshadowed by anxiety, because I'd realized where we were going next, where we *had* to go next, and I wasn't sure how Zelda would take it.

"That was marvelous, Parker," she said, leaning over and resting her head against my shoulder. "But I hope you didn't only do that because of what I said, about your being arrested. I mean, I hope you did it for your own sake and not for mine."

I squeezed her hand, as if in agreement.

"So, where to next?"

I didn't answer. She only began to understand when we crested the hill and the hospital came into view.

"Wait. Why are we here?"

I pulled to a stop in a loading zone and pointed toward the door. *Your turn,* I signed, forgetting she didn't understand the language.

"What?"

I opened up my journal. *Your turn,* I wrote.

"My turn?" She laughed condescendingly. "This isn't a game, Parker. There are no 'turns.'"

Why not? I did what I had to do. Now you have to.

"I don't have to do anything!"

She seemed a little ashamed of her own intensity, and when she spoke again, her voice was calmer. "Parker, I'm very proud of you for all the progress you've made, but my situation is entirely different from yours. Your father has been gone for years. My husband is still alive."

Not really. You said it yourself.

"But . . ." She ran out of argument before she'd even begun to argue. "But I can't."

I turned to two fresh pages in the Moleskine.

Now, I wrote on one.

Never, I wrote on the other.

I held the journal up, and Zelda stared at it for a few seconds. "That's a cliché," she said.

I shook the journal.

"I know!" she shouted. Then, more quietly, "I know." She closed her eyes and took a deep breath. "Stay here, all right? I have to do this alone." She opened the door but turned back to look at me. "Thank you, Parker. For everything."

I watched her pass through the sliding doors of the hospital. The rain was still coming down, but the sun had emerged from behind the clouds out over the water. There'd probably be a rainbow.

Suddenly something underneath me started shaking, and because I live in San Francisco (and because I was pretty keyed up in general at this point), I assumed it was an earthquake. I jumped out of the car, only to realize that the shaking was localized right around the area of my new, too-tight jeans: my phone was vibrating.

You have to understand, no one *ever* calls me (for reasons that are probably pretty easy to work out), so I wasn't used to the sensation. Still, I had a pretty good idea who it would be. My mom must have gotten home and noticed all the missing pictures, not to mention the missing car. I thought about ignoring her, but then I figured, fuck it. Today was a day for *not* ignoring things.

"Hello?" she said. "You're there, right? If you're there, tap your finger against the speaker." She didn't sound angry yet, but that could very well be a temporary situation.

Tap.

"You have the car? Tap once for yes and twice for no."

Tap.

"And you're with Zelda?"

Tap.

"Okay. Good." She gave a relieved sigh. "I just wanted to make sure it wasn't stolen."

Tap tap.

A long pause. I pulled the phone away from my ear to see if the call was still going.

"You know the Shakespeare Garden, in the park?"

Tap.

"I spent the morning walking around the neighborhood, and I ended up there. I actually talked to Shakespeare a bit. I mean, not the real Shakespeare—I'm not completely cuckoo yet—but that statue of him. He has a very reassuring presence. Then I came home, and I saw what you'd done, and I decided to call. So here I am." She sounded strange, like a kid almost, and I remembered something Zelda had told me once: *No one ever really stops feeling young.* "I'm sorry about yesterday, Parker. I shouldn't have gotten so angry. I just . . . I felt like something was finally shifting these past few days. You went to that party, and you have a—well, whatever Zelda is to you—and you're planning to go to college. And then you got into that fight at the movie theater, and it was like everything was going back to the way it's been. And that was hard for me because . . . well . . . because I've been a pretty shitty parent." No amount of tapping could serve as an adequate response to that, so I just waited. "I know that. I'm guilty of a little wallowing. I drink too much. And yes, sometimes I idealize your father. It's hard not to. Not because he was so great all the time—which he wasn't, by the way—but because that's just what happens when people die. They sorta get the red carpet treatment, because they can't disappoint you anymore. And you can't be mad at a dead person, because being mad takes a lot of fuel, you know? And where are you gonna get that fuel now that they're gone? So all you have left is all that love, even when you don't want it anymore. Well, that and a bunch of photographs." She paused. "Did you throw them away?"

Tap.

"I figured. I thought about doing it myself a million times before. I really did. But to take them all down, to really commit to that—it felt like killing him all over again. That's the thing about letting someone go. It's a kind of murder. Or more like a murder-suicide. You have to kill the person in your memory and then you have to kill the version of you that needed that person. It's big, Parker. And I just haven't been big enough to do it. Hey, are you okay?"

Somewhere along the line, I'd started crying, and I guess my mom heard me sniffle.

Tap.

"We can talk about it more later, okay?"

Tap.

"You're still in trouble for that fight, by the way. You don't get a free pass just because I'm apologizing. I'm still your mom."

Tap.

"Oh, and you can bring Zelda to dinner if you want. I'll be nice."

Tap.

"Okay. I'll see you later."

I hung up. The sun was completely out now over the Bay, scattering spangles across the water, though it stubbornly kept on raining where I was. If I'd been able to speak, I would've told my mom that I agreed with everything she'd said, except for one thing: I don't think that there's such a thing as "letting go." Like, I don't know much about the brain, but I do know that everything sticks in there; we've yet to develop the *Eternal Sunshine of the Spotless Mind* technology to delete the stuff we don't want to have to think about anymore. And that means that everything you've ever seen and heard and felt, along with everyone you've ever loved (and hated, and wanted, and wanted to hate and hated to want) is locked in your brain until the day you die. So why would the heart be any different? I don't think we should ever expect to let go. We just have to move on anyway.

And that made me think about Zelda, and what she was about to do. The optimist inside me said maybe everything really had turned around for her in just a few days, the way it had for me. But I'm not really a very optimistic person.

How long had she been gone? Only ten minutes, maybe fifteen. But I felt a cold bubble of dread forming in my stomach, because suddenly I knew she wasn't coming back. I left the car double-parked and unlocked and ran toward the hospital. The homeless man in the Yale sweatshirt was still camped out by the hospital door, but I heard him cackling at the same time I saw the crumpled wad of bills in his hand.

Nathaniel's room was empty but for Nathaniel: the only guy in San Francisco who spoke less than I did. *Beep. Beep.*

I went to the nurse's desk on the seventh floor and reached across to steal a pad of Post-its.

"Whatchoo doin'?" the nurse asked.

Was a girl just in here? I wrote.

"You mean the one with the weird hair?"

I nodded.

"Yeah. She spoke with Dr. Romaniello."

And then?

"Beats me. She left."

My mom's car already had a ticket on it, but it fluttered out from under the windshield wiper like some huge moth as I tore out of the spot. Zelda must've gone out a back entrance and called a car. It meant she had a head start on me, but not much of one. And luckily—and unluckily—I knew exactly where she was going.

THE BRIDGE

THE RAIN LET UP SOMEWHERE ALONG THE way to the Golden Gate Bridge. I'd always wondered about that threshold, between where it was raining and where it wasn't. Somewhere, that line had to exist, didn't it? You'd be standing in one place and getting rained on, then you'd step a couple inches to the side, and the rain would be gone. Even if it let up gradually, so gradually that you couldn't even tell it was happening, there had to be one final step that took you out of the shadow of the clouds and into the sunlight.

I drove across the city as fast as I could, rolling through stop signs and running through intersections after the light turned red. If a cop had spotted me, he probably would've had a chase on his hands, but I made it to the water unopposed. I ran through the wet grass of the park at the base of the bridge, past the cross-sectioned sample of the Golden Gate's suspension cable and a few tourists giving peace signs for the camera.

Up on the span, there didn't look to be anyone else around, except for the occasional bicycle whizzing by, its rider as lean and arched as a greyhound. I started walking, hoping I wasn't too late. Cars rumbled over the metal gratings. In the distance, rain clouds went on doing their usual wetwork, but the sun was bright and glary here.

"They tried to build an antisuicide barrier, you know." She'd been hidden, or maybe even hiding, behind one of the tall red stanchions at the center of the bridge. As I passed by, she began to speak. I might not have noticed her if she hadn't. "This was back in the seventies. But they couldn't make it happen. You know why? Because people thought it would be too ugly. It's just not the Golden Gate Bridge if it's all covered in safety nets and railings." Zelda crossed the narrow cement sidewalk and leaned out over the edge, gazing down at the flecked blackness of the bay. "Now, you might think it really doesn't matter one way or the other—if a person wants to kill herself, she'll just find some other way to do it, right? Wrong. It turns out that most people make these decisions pretty lightly, on the spur of the moment, and if they can't do it at the precise moment when the thought occurs, they often don't do it at all." She stepped up onto the lower bar of the railing. I went to stand next to her.

That's pretty fucked up, I wrote in my Moleskine.

"Is it? I learned about all this more than three decades ago, and I still haven't decided. On the one hand, yes, it sounds terrible to value some old bridge over a human life. But on the other hand, why *should* a human life be worth more than the beauty of this bridge? A lot of people died to build it, you know, and they died so that it would look like this. And it's lasted a lot longer than your average person does. So maybe it *is* more important."

Maybe. Just don't jump off it.

"Speak to me, Parker. Speak a single word and I won't."

That's not fair.

"It's as fair as what you're asking." She went up on her tiptoes, and I noticed the delicately scalloped skin between her heel and ankle. She put her elbows on the railing. My whole body was tensed, ready to spring forward and pull her back if it came to that. "So how would you do it, if you had to?"

Do what?

"Off yourself."

I frowned. *I haven't thought about it.*

"Of course you have. Everyone has."

She was right, of course. I mimed throwing back a handful of pills.

Zelda gave a measured nod. "Pharmaceuticals can be good. But difficult to keep them down. People always underestimate the lifesaving power of regurgitation." Now she began to lean forward, folding all the way over the bar, so that she looked like a towel on a rack. "I told them to let Nathaniel go," she said. "And you were right. It felt good. I mean, not *good* good, but, you know, good. And then I came here. I could've done it already, you know. But I decided to wait. I couldn't leave you without a real goodbye."

You don't have to leave at all, I wrote, in big scrawled letters. *I changed everything about myself so you'd stay. What was the point of all that if you go?*

She must have heard me writing, but she stayed bent over the railing, so she couldn't see what I'd written.

"You're the best thing that's happened to me in a lifetime, Parker. Maybe two. I'm a very lucky girl."

I leaned way out over the water, so I could hold my journal in front of her face, and I felt my feet lift up off the sidewalk and my weight shift forward. In another couple of seconds, I would've gone over myself. But Zelda had sensed what was happening. She straightened up just in time to pull me back onto the path. I scrabbled for the railing and dropped the notebook in the process. It flipped end over end, splashing silently into the water: *Now, Never, Now, Never.*

Then Zelda was hugging me so tightly it felt like the wind had been knocked out of me. She put her lips inside the whorl of my ear and whispered. "It's been quite an adventure, hasn't it?"

She let me go. And I hummed as hard as I could, just as I'd been taught to do in Dr. Joondeph's office, just as I'd done in that dream. I was aiming for *I love you.* What I got was: "Mm Mmm Mmm."

Zelda laughed. "Not a word, Parker Santé, but a fine finale. Look out!"

She pointed behind me. I turned, expecting one of those crazy bicyclists to come whizzing by like a bullet train. But there was only the long empty pathway, still sparkling from the rain. When I turned back around, Zelda had risen to stand on the railing, one hand on the metal post beside her. None of the cars on the bridge so much as slowed down, but I swear time itself did. Her silver hair was whipping around in the wind as if each strand were alive, her sea-green eyes spilling rivers down her cheeks. I remembered the first time I saw her, sitting alone in the dining room of the Palace Hotel, tapping at her egg. Perfect sadness. Silver, not platinum. And every moment of our time together suddenly came back to me, in pointillist bursts of color: Elbows touching on a movie-theater armrest. The angels' share. Genmaicha. Still life. Cherry Icee. A stolen scarf. *Beep.* Moleskine. Columbia University. The hydra. Skin and more skin. *Crack.* Flutter. And all of it bringing us here, to this frozen instant on the Golden Gate Bridge. She looked back at me, one last time, and the sadness I saw in her face was different from the sadness I'd seen that first day. *Imperfect* sadness maybe, which was another way of saying there was a little splinter of happiness in there too. I'd given her that at least.

And then she jumped.

AFTERWARD

AND

AFTERWORD

GOODBYE, BANANA

THE BANANA WAS GONE.

It had been replaced with a painting of a couple wrapped up in a checkered quilt of gold and cream and black. My first thought was that the banana must have been stolen, but of course that was ridiculous. Who would steal a giant picture of a banana? Then again, who would buy it in the first place? The world was full of mysteries.

"You looking for the banana?" Dr. Milton said. "I figured it was time for a change. Got some Klimt instead."

"What banana?" my mom asked.

"Just something I used to have on the wall."

"Oh." My mom laughed awkwardly. "I thought it was some kind of expression."

She was there as part of what I liked to call "the self-improvement super package": joint therapy, individual therapy (for both of us), AA for her, and speech therapy for me. It was weird, at first, seeing her in Dr. Milton's office. For half a decade, this had been the place I came to say all the things I couldn't say to her. But it was good in a way too. It was a change.

We didn't talk about anything specific—just whatever had been going on that week. There was a lot to talk about. I was finishing my applications, but I still wasn't convinced I wanted to go to college just yet. Why not take a year or two off to bum around a bit? Zelda had told me I ought to travel more, and it seemed stupid to go straight from twelve years of education to four more, without even doing anything to celebrate in between. Unsurprisingly, my mom disagreed. She and I still didn't agree on much of anything, when it came down to it. But it seemed to make her happy just to be talking about the future.

The future—that dirty rat bastard of a concept. It kept on coming. One week gone by. Then another. Then another.

"I don't even understand why they call it Alcoholics Anonymous," my mom said during one of our sessions. "It's not anonymous at all! People are always saying their name. 'I'm Marian, and I'm an alcoholic,' and then everyone goes, 'Hi, Marian!' It's about as un-anonymous as you can get."

You should make up a fake name, I signed.

"What about Catwoman? Can I be Catwoman?"

That would be weird.

"What about Zelda? That wasn't her real name, was it?"

It was Griselda, actually.

"Wow. Really? I've never known a Griselda. Fancy."

"Have you had any word from her?" Dr. Milton asked me. I shook my head. I'd told them she'd had to move away because her dad got a new job in Australia. If I'd told them the truth, I'd have ended up in therapy for the rest of my life. Or maybe a straitjacket.

"What a shame," my mom said. "I owe so much to that girl. I'd like to take her out for a nice dinner."

Me too, I signed.

"A few days ago, this song came on the radio. It's by Leonard Cohen. I forget the name—something about a raincoat?"

"'Famous Blue Raincoat,'" Dr. Milton said.

"Yeah, that one. There's a line in it, um . . ." She hummed a little bit, then found the thread of the melody. "*'Thanks for the trouble you took from her eyes. I thought it was there for good, so I never tried.'* You know that one, Parker?" I shook my head. "It's so beautiful. Anyway, that's how I feel about Zelda. She took the trouble, you know?"

Sounds like a good song, I signed.

In the weeks after Zelda jumped, I spent a lot of time at this café down by the water, writing in my journal or else cobbling together some pathetic excuse of a history paper at the last minute. When I was done, I'd walk to the beach, then north along the shoreline, to where the waves slammed into the rocks below Cliff House, sending up columns of spume like the spray from a whale's blowhole.

One afternoon I ran into Alana up there. Though I passed her in the halls at school all the time, we hadn't had an actual conversation since the day of the multiplex brawl. I'd been avoiding her, to be honest. I guess seeing her reminded me of that weekend, which reminded me of Zelda.

She was sitting on the beach, reading some textbook. She hadn't noticed me, so I still would have had time to turn around and go back the other way, if I'd wanted to.

She didn't look up when I sat down next to her.

"Hi," I said.

That got her attention.

"Did you just say hi?"

I got out my cell phone. *It's the only word I know,* I typed.

I'd been doing that humming exercise for an hour a day for the last month, and so far the total payoff was just that one word—"hi"—which is barely more than a hum anyway.

"Well, it's a good one," she said. "It reminds me of a joke. You wanna hear it?"

I nodded.

"So a guy brings a dog into the auditions for *America's Got Talent*. And one of the judges is like, 'So what's your act?' And the guy says, 'My dog can talk.' The judges all look at each other, pretty skeptical, obviously. 'Let's see it,' says the first judge. So the guy turns to his dog and he says, 'Hey, Fido, what do you call the thing on top of a house?' And the dog goes, 'Ruff!' And then the guy says, 'That's right, Fido. And remind me, what's the opposite of smooth again?' And the dog goes, 'Ruff!' And then the guy goes, 'Good boy! And now, why don't you tell me how masochists like to be treated in the bedroom.' And the dog goes, 'Ruff!' By now, the judges are waving their hands for this guy to stop. 'Get the hell out of here,' they say. 'You and your dog are full of shit.' So the guy and the dog leave the room, and once they're outside, the dog goes, 'On second thought, do you think I should have said "like the dirty little bitches they are"?'"

I laughed. Before I'd met Zelda, I'd hated to laugh in front of people. But somewhere along the line, I'd stopped caring whether I looked weird when I did it.

"What I'm thinking is that maybe we can make this work for you, too, Parker. Like, check it—how do you feel after you take a big bong hit?"

I raised an eyebrow. What was she getting at?

"Just say the one word you know, okay? How do you feel after you take a big bong hit?"

"Hi," I said.

"Interesting. And what kind of school did you go to after middle school?"

"High," I said, finally getting the joke.

"Correct again. And Thom Yorke of Radiohead definitely doesn't want to be left dry. Remind me, what else doesn't he want to be left?"

"High," I said.

Then we were both laughing, though the only sound was Alana's laughter, dying out beneath the smashing of the waves and the cawing of the gulls. Those birds always made me think of *Finding Nemo*, where it turns out the only thing that seagulls are ever saying is *Mine!*, over and over again. That's one of the things I've learned, living without speech for so long. No matter what someone actually says, all they're ever *really* saying is this: *Me! Me! Pay attention to me! I exist! I matter!*

"That's what I always liked about you, Parker," Alana said. "You know when to shut up. I could really learn something from you. So let's just sit here and shut up together, yeah? I'd really like that."

And so we did. Eventually we lay back on the sand, staring up at the sun, wordless, side by side.

STORY #4:
ACCEPTANCE

I HAVE NOT, AS OF THE TYPING OF THIS sentence, ended up with Alana. Later that same day, she told me she'd met someone new a couple of weeks earlier. At a chess tournament, if you can believe that.

"He's just as big a nerd as me," she said proudly.

So this is not a story of love triumphing over all, or one where the boy gets the girl. In fact, it's not really a story at all. But you know that already, don't you?

Whatever decision you make, I'd love to know if this is the longest response to an essay question you've ever received. I figured that with my one recommendation, my terrible grades, and my criminal record, I'd have to go above and beyond *somehow*. So I chose to go exactly 60,209 words above and beyond. The good news is we're almost done. Bear with me for just a couple more pages.

It's funny. When I started working on this essay, sitting in front of a computer in the library computer lab while my friends tried to distract me with Call of Duty, I felt a weird sort of disappointment. How could anything in my life ever measure up to what I'd just been through? I mean, meeting

Zelda was magic, wasn't it? And not just your typical "Oh I'm so in love oh my God isn't it fucking AMAZING?" magic. This was *real* magic. And now there was just the *real* left, for the rest of my life probably.

But now that I've written it all down, I've gotten a little bit of perspective on all the dots, and I'm starting to connect them. I think maybe the closest thing we mortals get to magic is just change. Alana getting a nerdy boyfriend. My mom coming to therapy. Me humming my way into "hi." And I really do understand why Zelda did what she did. We all spend our lives as the rope in a game of tug-of-war. On one side, you've got the weight of the unchangeable past pulling at you, and on the other, you've got the unpredictable future. If you're lucky, you stay balanced right in the middle. But if you're unlucky (and I think most of us are, some of the time anyway), you end up falling over one way or the other. Zelda had more past pulling at her than anyone, but I think it was the future that finally killed her. A future that stretched out in front of her forever, no matter which way she turned, like the view from the center of the Sahara. *No doy mas. Ya basta.* Still life. When change loses its magic, then there really isn't anything left to live for. So that's my new mantra. Keep changing. I've stopped hanging out in hotels. They're all the same, anyway. I'm trying to spend more time with other human beings. It isn't always easy. Like Zelda said, people can be so stupid, it's a wonder they manage to keep breathing. But if I can just get them to shut up, to lie back on a beach with me for five measly minutes, I think I can keep it together.

And I wouldn't blame you for thinking this whole story has been a bunch of BS—just another fairy tale, like all the others. Maybe I've never met someone named Zelda, but I thought a good yarn might distract you from how unqualified I am to attend your illustrious institution. Or maybe I met a girl who was magical in a more traditional, not-actually-magical way, and so I used the power of fiction to transform her into something bigger and more profound. Or maybe I met a girl who claimed to have lived for two hundred and forty-six years, and though I never actually believed her, I went along with it because she was hot.

But you have to allow for the possibility, however tiny, that I really *did* meet a girl who was born in 1770 in Kassel, Germany, and over the course of a weekend she transformed my life, even though I didn't manage to transform hers, and I've set down the story here because it's the truth. And if you don't believe it, well, that's your own business, because in the end, it doesn't really matter one way or the other. You don't have to decide whether the story I've told you is true. You only have one decision to make, don't you?

I'll be awaiting your reply. Take your time.

ACKNOWLEDGMENTS

To Christian, Justin, Lizzy, Chrissy, Katy, Jenica, Chava,
and the whole team at Simon & Schuster . . .
To John and everyone at Folio and Greenhouse . . .
To Mom, Seth, Bobby D., Tallie, Casey, Giulio, Sean,
and all the friends and family who have put up with me . . .
To the staff of the MacDowell Colony, where this book
was finished, then rewritten from scratch . . .
To the many authors I've gotten to know over the last year,
who have so kindly inducted me into this brave new world . . .
And to the many readers who have reached out and said hello
(or just tattooed an asteroid on their wrist) . . .
Thanks for the trouble.